COOLER

© 2017 by

DAVID MALCOLM ROSE

davidmalcolmrose(at)yahoo(dot)com

Cover art by Ike Garlington

OTHER BOOKS BY
DAVID MALCOLM ROSE

TUPELO STREET

THE ROCK & ROLL CHRONICLES

COOLER

STATE STREET BLUES

WOODSTOCK BEFORE WOODSTOCK

SEEDS AND STEMS

BIG BOX BLUES – A 2 ACT PLAY

CHAPTER 1

Edward Eliot Emmons enjoyed his life ... mostly. He enjoyed his school and his neighborhood, and this was important because when he wasn't in one, he was usually in the other. He enjoyed his house, in no small part because he had his own room and didn't have to share with his younger brother, Clemens. He enjoyed his bicycle, his soccer team, and his books. Most of all he enjoyed his computer and the many places it could take him. Getting on his computer was like entering a magical world that was all his own. What was even better, it was a world he could control.

There were some things he did not enjoy as much: haircuts, piano lessons and Brussels sprouts were high on that list. There was one thing, however, that Edward did not care for in the least, and that was the very thing he was doing right then, at that very moment. He was grocery shopping with his father and brother, and that was just no fun at all. And this was not just a small neighborhood grocery store they were in, this was BUY-N-BULK. It was huge, and you could get anything here from cat food to car parts, from fruit juice to farm implements. And this was not just a normal trip to the market. Thanksgiving was coming up, and the list of things they needed to get was especially long.

Shopping seemed to take forever because his father was very thorough and insisted on reading the labels on everything he put into the cart. The labels were long and often very complicated, and Edward's father was constantly worrying about grams of this, ounces of that, and percentages of something else entirely. Was a particular product low in sugar, high in fiber, low in fat, high in protein, and what date was it best used before? And the store's motto, "More Than You'll Ever Use for Less Than You'd Expect", did nothing to speed the process along. It seemed like every item was bundled in shrink wrap bunches of two or three or four. Edward's father had to do a lot of math to decide which package was the best bargain.

The aisles in the grocery store were numbered, and Edward mentally crossed them off one by one as if he were a prisoner crossing off the years until his release. Clemens, his brother, was no help whatsoever. Just when they made it to the end of one aisle and his father was through counting grams, figuring ounces, and adding up percentages, his brother would run up with a box, bag, or bottle of something and try to slip it into the shopping cart.

Clemens would always do this on the turns from one aisle to the next. While their father was concentrating on the specials that were displayed on the end cap, his little brother would try to sneak an item over the edge and into the basket. He was always caught.

Their father, an agreeable man by nature, would laugh at Clemens and then give the item a proper review. He would carefully check all the information on the label and then declare the item either a necessity, a reward, or something that needed to be returned to the shelf from which it came. All this would take time, and Edward, who was anxious to cross the aisle off his mental list, would simply have to wait.

Today's journey was a long one. Edwards did not understand how they could be out of so many things when both the refrigerator and the cabinets in the kitchen at home all appeared to be full. But the end was near. They had gotten eggs and juice at the back of the store and covered the meat and cheese section down the side. They had endured endless aisles of cereals, chips, soups, breads, and household cleaners. They even found the peanut butter and the frozen ravioli on the first try, a feat that had never been accomplished before. And now here they were in the fruit and vegetable section. The checkout stands, like shining lights at the end of the tunnel, were in view.

Edward's father ran his finger down the shopping list he had brought from home. One by one he clicked off the items with the efficiency of a computerized machine. "All we have to get now is celery, carrots, bananas and ... Oh polliwogs! I've forgotten the milk," he said.

"Edward, you know the kind of milk we drink, in the jug with the red label. Could you go get us a gallon?"

Edward's heart fell. He did not want to go. Stopping what he was doing and moving on to something else had long been a problem for him. Getting into the bath, getting out of the bath; going to bed, getting up; all these changes were, and always had been, difficult for Edward. And now he would have to stop moving forward and start moving back.

What made it even worse was that they were so close to the end. He could see past the checkout counters, out through the glass doors, and into the parking lot beyond. He could see the finish line; he could see freedom.

He could also see his brother Clemens sneaking up to the shopping cart with a marked down, surplus, Halloween pumpkin that was almost as big as he was. The younger Emmons was on his tip toes and straining to get the pumpkin over the lip of the cart. It was not going to be a soft landing what with all the other items already in the basket. From Edward's view point it looked like the eggs and corn chips were goners for sure and a loaf of bread was about to be squished down until each slice was the size of a soda cracker. Delay was inevitable. Edward went to get the milk.

"Don't forget to check the expiration date," his father called after him. "Get a gallon from the very back of the cooler."

Edward already knew about checking the expiration date. He didn't need to be told. After all, he was practically 11 years old, well, ten and a half anyway. The big problem was that the milk was in one of the coolers which were way at the back, just about the furthermost point it could possibly be and still be in the store, at least on the grocery side. He started off walking as fast as he could, almost at a trot. He turned a corner and nearly ran into a very large lady who was riding in a motorized shopping cart. A store employee, with nut brown pants and a brown nylon vest with iridescent stripes, gave the boy a cautionary look and pointed a price checking tool as if it were a ray gun. Edward slowed his pace and then thought about his father and Clemens who by now were probably cleaning broken eggs off the pumpkin. He slowed down even more to a leisurely walk, and a smile came across his face.

Nearly the entire back wall of the store was covered with a line of tall, glass-fronted coolers whose shelves were stocked with cheese and yogurt, margarine and sour cream. He passed the almond milk and wondered how difficult it would be to get milk from an almond and how many nuts it would take to make a quart. After that was the soy milk. His father had once stopped near a field outside of town and showed his sons how soybeans grew. They had picked some and peeled the yellow beans from their fuzzy pod. They were even smaller than almonds, much smaller.

There was butter milk, chocolate milk, strawberry milk and whipped cream in tubs and spray cans, and cartons of cream that were not whipped at all. After the cream came Half and Half and then coffee creamers of every flavor, some of which looked so good as to make Edward wish he were old enough to drink coffee. Eventually the shelves gave over to more conventional milk. There was low-fat milk, no-fat milk, 1% milk, 2% milk and skim milk. There was color everywhere: milk in white jugs with blue labels and milk in yellow jugs with purple labels, lactose free milk in orange cartons, and organic milk in green cartons with smiling, happy cows on the front.

Edward had been down this row many times before, but with all the choices and all the colors he was now feeling a bit uncomfortable. The truth was, Edward never did feel entirely comfortable with the coolers. The problem wasn't with the countless milk products or the wire shelves, the problem was with the void beyond. As much as he tried, he was never able to see what was back beyond the products and the shelving. When he put his face up close to the doors his breath steamed up the glass. When he opened the door, the chilled air steamed up his glasses.

The further reaches of the coolers had always been a mystery to Edward, and he was not a huge fan of mystery. When he was young, he imagined that there were cows back there in that moon-dark landscape with farmers milking them as fast as they could, trying to keep up with the demand. What lay beyond the cows was anybody's guess.

He finally found what he was looking for, whole milk in a jug with a red label. He was happy to see the milk he sought was on one of the middle shelves where he could reach it, but there didn't seem to be many gallons left, and those were set to expire in just a few days. Thanksgiving shoppers had been hitting the store hard.

Edward was about to give up and take one of the remaining milk jugs when he spotted, pushed way toward the back, a single gallon with a red label. The jug was turned just right, and the expiration date was visible. It was a good one.

He reached in as far as he could, but the plastic jug was slippery. When he tried to grab it, it squirted from his fingers and farther back into the cooler. The jug was now as far back as it could go without falling off the wire shelf. In fact, it was teetering on the distant edge.

Edward put his foot up on the lower ledge of the cooler and slid himself as far into the slot between the two shelves as he could. This was the farthest back into the cooler he had ever been, the farthest anybody had ever been as far as he knew. He tried to look around and see what was past the jug, but the shelves were too close together, and he could not turn his head enough to see. Besides, his glasses were as foggy as a London street.

Reaching up with one hand he managed to hook his fingers into the plastic handle of the jug. And then an odd thing happened. The bottom ledge of the cooler was damp with condensation, his foot slipped. At the same time, the gallon jug fell off the back of the shelf. Edward's finger became stuck in the plastic handle of the milk jug. He was pulled into the cooler, across the shelf, and down into the darkness beyond. The last thing he heard was the cooler door clicking shut behind him.

CHAPTER TWO

Edward sat up with his back against the inside of the wire shelves and looked around. The light coming down from the two small bulbs high on the ceiling was dim at best. His glasses were hopelessly fogged by the chilly air in the cooler. He took off his specks, but his blurry vision was worse than the fog. He wiped his glasses clean on his shirt tail and put them back on. The fog quickly began to form again; but in the few seconds before it clouded his vision entirely, he saw what he believed to be a garden Gnome perched high on top of a stack of plastic milk crates in a distant corner. This was an odd place, Edward thought, to keep a garden Gnome.

Edwards fingers began to feel cold and then a chill spread to the end of his nose. His glasses began to cool off as well, and the fog disappeared. He was in a long, narrow room that ran the length of the cooler. The only illumination, other than the two small bulbs, was the light that filtered in through the glass doors at the front of the cooler and past the cartons and jugs of milk. The back wall was stacked with plastic crates, some empty and some full of milk and milk products. He did not see anything that looked like a garden Gnome which was, in a way, a relief. At both ends of the room were solid doors with large hinges and long, stainless steel handles.

Edward stood up and, for the first time, noticed that the gallon milk jug was still stuck on his hand. He tried to free his fingers, but they were wedged in tightly. He would need help. He was sure his father could solve this problem; his father was very good at such things. The gallon jug was just what they needed, and all he had to do was get it to the front of the store. His father would take it from there.

He got up and walked over to the closest door, the one on the milk end of the cooler as opposed to the cheese and yogurt end. The stainless-steel latch was mounted up high on the door and, while Edward could reach it, he could not get enough leverage to pull it open. The gallon jug, which seem to be permanently attached to his hand, was not helpful at all. Edward stacked several empty milk crates against the door and found that by standing on the crates he was tall enough and could get the needed leverage to pull the latch open. Unfortunately, while he could pull the latch, he could not open the door because the crates on which he was standing were in the way. It was what his father would refer to as a Catch-22. Without the crates, he wasn't tall enough to operate the latch, and with the crates he couldn't open the door. It was becoming apparent that the only other way out of the room was the way by which he entered.

Edward went back over to the wire shelves and looked out at the glass doors beyond. All he would have to do would be to crawl across the nearly empty shelf he came in on. Once he got to the door at the front, he could push it open and tumble out into the main part of the store. It would be difficult with the gallon jug still stuck on his hand, but he was confident he could do it.

Edward brought a milk crate over in front of the wire shelves, got up on it, and began to crawl into the slot. The shelves were cold and damp from condensation. At first he tried to push the milk jug ahead of him but soon found that to be cumbersome. He crawfished around until he was sideways on the shelf and the plastic jug was behind him. From there he could reach the glass door with his free hand. Edward pushed the door, but it did not move. He worked his body around until he got one foot against the door and pushed with all his strength, but the door wouldn't budge. Edward realized that the latches on the glass cooler doors were meant to be opened from the outside. No one could have imagined a situation where someone crawling across the shelves from the inside would need to open one of the doors. There was not even so much as a handle on the inside.

Edward did not deal with transition well and he did not deal with departure from the norm very well either. What he wanted from his life was smooth progress from one event to the next, and this was not shaping up to be anything at all like that. Adventure, while a fine subject to read about, was quite a different matter when it came to living it. He remembered his father's teachings. He took a few deep breaths, closed his eyes, and told himself not to panic. Panicking would be of no use whatsoever. He would simply crawl back to the long room behind the shelves and find another way out of the cooler. He contorted his body even further and began to maneuver back the way he had come. Almost immediately the gallon jug tipped at an angle and hung up between the top and bottom wire shelves. He could not get it to move in or out. He could not even see it clearly because his jacket had worked its way up over his head.

Right now, Edward Eliot Emmons thought, would be a good time to panic. He turned his head back toward the glass door and began to yell for help. The only thing this accomplished was to steam up the glass. Edward gathered his wits about him and wrote HELP in the fog that covered the window. He thought about it and realized that what he had written would be seen as backwards from the other side. He hastily wiped it out, breathed out heavily to fog the glass once again, and wrote PLEH.

He was admiring his handy work when it occurred to him that even PLEH was wrong. All the letters, with the exception of the H, would be backwards. He took his hand, wiped out the letters, and once again tried to fog up the glass. But now there was too much oil from his fingers on the surface, and the fog was patchy at best.

Through the patchy fog Edward could see a man coming his way. He could only see the man from the waist to the knees but, judging by the nut-brown work pants, he was sure it was a BUY-N-BULK employee. The man was pushing a large bucket mounted on wheels with a mop and a ringer inside. Edward began to pound on the glass with the flat of his hand and yell at the top of his lungs. The man in the brown pants passed on by. Edward twisted his neck as far as he could to watch, but the man passed out of sight. Edward rested his head on the wire shelf and took stock of the situation. He was very cold, very stuck, and very, very scared.

CHAPTER 3

"Butter."

It was a rather silly and giggling voice, but Edward heard the word clearly. Unfortunately, with his head, and his whole body for that matter, stuck between the shelves, he could not tell from which direction the voice came. He tried looking around to identify the speaker; but in his current situation, with his jacket obscuring his vision, it was hopeless.

"Butter."

This time the boy could tell the voice was coming from the long narrow room behind the cooler shelves. Edward looked at the glass doors in front of him. In the reflection he could see back into the room behind the shelves, the room he was trying to escape. There was a garden Gnome there for sure, and the Gnome was watching him with a bemused smile. At least Edward thought the Gnome was watching him, it was hard to tell because the little man's eyes were hidden behind a pair of heavy-framed, dark, sunglasses.

"What do you mean by butter?" Edward said. "I should think I have more pressing needs than preparing biscuits."

The garden Gnome did not respond but turned and passed out of Edward's limited field of vision.

"Come back! Come back! Where are you going? I really could use a little help here," Edward cried.

But the Gnome was gone. Edward was growing very stiff from lying motionless on the metal shelves. He worked his fingers and toes and tried to come up with a solution to his problem, but all he could think about was the garden Gnome. He had seen Gnomes before, in people's yards and among their plantings, but those didn't walk around, and they surely didn't talk. And why was this one so preoccupied with butter? Edward closed his eyes, partly to rest and partly to clear his mind.

He was working the problem over from every angle when he felt something slimy on his fingers, the fingers that were stuck in the jug's handle. He looked around, as best he could, and saw the garden Gnome applying butter to Edward's hand and the handle of the jug. The Gnome, clearly enjoying his work, giggled as he slathered butter all over the jug and halfway up to Edward's elbow. When the stick of butter was worn well down, the Gnome tossed it over his shoulder, grabbed hold of the jug, and said "Pull!"

The boy pulled with all his might. The little man pulled as well, and the jug came free of Edwards hand. The Gnome fell backwards out of Edward's vision and the gallon milk jug went over the edge as well.

"Are you okay!" Edward called with great concern.

By way of answer the garden Gnome popped back up into the boy's vision. His hat was askew, and milk drip from the point of his beard.

"I would guess you could get out by yourself now," the Gnome giggled. "Be careful so you don't slip in the milk and butter."

Edward worked his way out from between the shelves and back down onto the milk crate. "You look to be a garden Gnome, and yet you can talk," he said. "What's up with that?"

"I am not just any old garden Gnome, I am a Free Gnome, we are a proud and noble people," the Gnome said. "Don't the Gnomes on the BUY-N-BULK side talk?"

"Not as a rule. In fact, I've never known one to walk around or even to move at all for that matter."

The little man removed his scarf and wrung the milk out. "That must be a dreadful place for Gnomes. Makes me happy to be living on the side I'm living on."

The boy extended his hand to the Gnome. "By the way, my name is Edward."

The Gnome draped his wet scarf over Edward's butter-coated hand. "My name is Sebastian Lorenzo Ignacio Nathaniel Kincaid."

Edward accepted the scarf and meticulously began wiping the butter from his arm and fingers. "That's a rather long name," he pointed out.

"Gnomes, at least Free Gnomes, here on the STUFF-4-LESS side, have a tendency toward long names."

"Sebastian Lorenzo Illogical ...," Edward started to say the Gnome's name but soon lost his way.

"Sebastian Lorenzo Ignacio Nathaniel Kinkaid," the Gnome stated. "But don't fret about it. Free Gnomes usually go by their initials."

"S.L.I.N.K.'" Edward said as he handed the buttery scarf back to the Gnome. "But doesn't that spell...."

"Slink. That's right," The Gnome said as he took the scarf in his fingertips and tossed it on the floor in the puddle of milk. "And you, Edward, must be a human. We've heard about humans over there on the BUY-IN-BULK side, but I've never seen one. I don't believe I've ever met a Gnome who has."

"You keep talking about sides, STUFF-4-LESS and BUY-N-BULK, but I'm not sure I know what that means."

Slink tilted his head and looked at Edward as if he was trying to figure out if the boy was putting him on. "They say that there are two sides to everything. This cooler looks to be the connection between the two," Slink began to explain as if talking to a small child. "We live in STUFF-4-LESS. That is our side, our Gnomeland," the little man pointed to the door at the far end of the cooler room. "While you, if I'm not mistaken, live in BUY-N-BULK," he said while pointing to the nearest door, the one Edward had been trying to open.

"Well, we don't exactly live in BUY-N-BULK," Edward corrected, "although sometimes it feels that way."

The Gnome removed his hat and wrung the milk out of it. "Our side is a highly advanced society. By all accounts I have heard, your side is rather primitive."

"If STUFF-4-LESS is such a wonderful place, then how come I've never heard of it before?" Edward said defensively. Who was this Gnome anyway? He was short, funny looking, and had milk in his beard.

"It's been said that BUY-N-BULKers lack the imagination to even consider the possibility that STUFF-4-LESS exists. I'm beginning to suspect that might be true."

Edward's first reaction was to come to the defense of his side, whichever that was, but he could think of little to say. Slink was right, he knew nothing of STUFF-4-LESS and, what's more, he didn't know anybody who did. His second thoughts were to deny the existence of the place. A few minutes ago, he could have done that; but now, standing here in conversation with a garden Gnome, he was finding that a hard position to maintain.

"My father has adjustable windshield wipers on his minivan," Edward said.

"Right," Slink said dismissively. "One of the great technological breakthroughs of your time I should guess."

"Look," the boy said. "I don't know about any of this. You say the STUFF-4-LESS is a wonderful place to live, and I'm sure it is. But all I want to do right now is to get some milk and get back to my side, wherever that is."

"Yes, I suspect you would. However so humble..." Slink began but, he got no farther.

The STUFF-4-LESS door, the door at the far end of the cooler, burst open. Bright light streamed in followed quickly by a motorized shopping cart driven by what looked like an oversized reptile with a head like a puffer fish. The monster had arms and hands with webbed fingers and legs with web-toed feet. On the front of the cart, extending below a basket loaded with food, was mounted a woodchipper with spinning blades. The creature aimed the cart, and the flashing blades of the chipper, right at Slink.

CHAPTER 4

Slink jumped quickly to the side, but just as quickly the creature spun his steering wheel in that direction. At the same time the monster took a loaf of frozen garlic bread from the pile of groceries in the basket of its cart and stuffed it into his mouth. The creature chomped down hard on the bread and stomped down hard on the gas pedal.

Just then the cart hit the butter and milk on the cooler floor. The machine went into a four-wheel drift, skidded the length of the room, and slammed hard up against the BUY-N-BULK door at the far end. The creature rocked violently sideways and hit its large, scaly head against the door making a hollow thudding sound like a pumpkin being dropped from a second story window onto the sidewalk. The motor on the cart coughed and died and so did the creature.

Edward could not take his eyes from the scene. The cart itself was uniquely equipped. The low-powered, electric motor, that was standard equipment on motorized shopping carts in BUY-N-BULK stores, had been replaced with a gasoline engine that must have come from a lawn mower. There were scabbards on either side that held large, sharp hand tools. The creature was even more extraordinary. Not only did it have the head of a sucker fish but a body that was extremely bloated, not unlike a toad. On its head was a helmet fashioned from a stew pot. The helmet was badly dented. The basket on the front of the cart was filled with all manner of food. The loaf of garlic bread protruded from the creature's mouth like a doughy thermometer.

"I think it choked to death on the bread," Edward said.

"That's the most common cause of death for Jamooks," Slink said as he picked through the remaining groceries in the basket on the front of the creature's cart.

"Jamooks?" Edward said.

"It's short for Fearonjamook," Slink replied. "You good with cupcakes, potato chips, cheese sticks and Double Cola? That's about all that's left here we can use, if you don't count two tins of sardines, which I don't."

Edward was almost in a trance. The Gnome's voice seemed to come from a great distance. He wanted to see if Slink was still in the cooler room but could not take his eyes from the creature in the cart. There was so much here that needed explaining. He had a million questions to ask, but only one came out. "Are the chips barbecue flavor?"

"Let's have a look. We have regular and sour cream," Slink said as he doubled up two of the shopping bags and began to load his swag.

Edward looked at the garden Gnome as if seeing him for the first time "Works for me," he said.

The Gnome threw the bag over his shoulder. "Grab his pricer and let's get out of here before we have more company."

"Pricer?"

"In the holster, on his belt," Slink said.

Edward looked at the midsection of the Jamook. There was a belt there, nearly obscured by rolls of fat. He found the holster and removed the pricer, which he thought looked just like the pricing tools used in BUY-N-BULK and other stores as well. He aimed it at a half gallon of chocolate milk on the cooler shelf and pulled the trigger. A green beam of light shot across the room and an explosion of milk filled the air. Much of it rained down on the Gnome. A hole, the shape of a crude dollar sign, smoldered in the side of what was left of the milk jug.

"This is getting tiresome," the Gnome said as he once again removed his hat and wrung out milk. "I don't know what pricers do on your side but in STUFF-4-LESS they're not toys."

Edward became conscious of the fact that he was now thinking in terms of sides. "I need to get back to my side before my father and brother begin to worry. That is, if they are not terribly worried already."

"That might be a problem. Your average Jamook has to weigh a good 300 pounds and the cart nearly as much," Slink said. "It would take us hours to move them before we could free the door, and we don't have hours. What we have is minutes, and not too many of them. It won't be long before more Jamooks come looking for this unfortunate fellow."

"But I can't go to STUFF-4-LESS," Edward said as he stuck the pricer in his jacket pocket and pulled at the cart with all his might. "I'm not a STUFF-4-LESSer, I'm a BUY-N-BULKer and proud to be one.

"Well, umm, we can just go around the other way," the Gnome said while trying to move Edward by pulling on his shirt tails. "That's just what we'll do. We'll go around to the other portal. It'll take us a while to get there, but it's much safer than staying here. Believe you-me, it's much, much safer."

The last of his words were lost to the deep rattle of an approaching engine. A second Jamook was coming to look for the first. Edward and Slink scurried behind the STUFF-4-LESS door just as a shadow fell across the opening. The second Jamook approached with caution; but, upon seeing his fallen comrade, revved his engine and lurched into the room.

Slink took Edward by the hand, and the two tiptoed out from behind the door. Edward looked back and watched as the second Jamook tried to free the garlic bread from the throat of Jamook number one. The bread was firmly wedged in place, and Jamook number two had to be content with breaking off the top part of the loaf and popping it into his own mouth. The second Jamook began sorting through the groceries in his departed cohort's cart as he chomped the bread so ravenously that crumbs and even large chunks flew from both sides of his mouth.

Edward had seen enough. He turned and, for the first time, looked out upon STUFF-4-LESS. What he saw was so startling that he stopped dead in his tracks. Slink, who was still holding his hand, was pulled up so short that he lost his footing, fell over backwards onto his sack and crushed the potato chips in the process. Edward, his mouth wide open, looked around in awe.

CHAPTER 5

What Edward saw before him was somewhat familiar and yet wholly foreign. It was a big box store, not unlike BUY-N-BULK, but a big box store gone terribly wrong. From his vantage point, which was admittedly quite restricted by towering mounds of broken baby toys which ran together with seemingly endless collapsed racks of shoes. Chaos and confusion seemed to be the order of the day.

The distant ceiling was much higher than any Edward had seen before in any store he'd ever been in. Light filtered down through the broken, kudzu-draped skylights. Crossing in front of them was a clear path through the rubbish that was easily wide enough for the motorized carts.

The air was almost tropical in nature and to Edward, after his ordeal in the cooler, it felt wonderfully warm. A tangle of artificial plants, both plastic and silk, dominated the foreground while a broken case of discarded candles spiced the air.

"Clean up in Section 1403," a loud voice came over the store intercom. It was a dark and threatening voice.

"We have to get off this Mook Trail as soon as possible," Slink said as he grabbed Edward's hand once again. "More Jamooks will be showing up any moment and there's always that one behind us in the portal to contend with."

They hurried down the trail for about 100 yards and then Slink suddenly stopped. Next to him, embedded in the wall of broken and discarded merchandise, was a battered TV stand. The Gnome looked both ways and then opened the doors in the front of the stand. "In you go," he said.

Edward squatted down and squinted into the opening. The shelves were gone from inside the stand, as was the back. Beyond that he could see a dimly lit tunnel leading away into complete darkness.

"Are you crazy?" Edward said. "I'm not crawling into that hole. I have no idea what's in there."

Slink turned his head sideways as if listening for distant sounds. Edward cocked his head as well. The Gnome was right. There was a sound out there, and it was growing closer. Edward was quite certain it was the sound of a lawnmower engine coming up the Mook Trail in their direction. The Gnome turned his head the other way, and Edward followed suit. The Jamook from the portal could be heard coming down the trail.

"You may not know what's in there, but I think you have a pretty good idea of what's out here," Slink said. "What you're hearing is the Jamook removal squad on the way. They pick up the dead and haul them off to the Mook Mincer."

"Mook Mincer?"

"It grinds up dead Jamooks for recycling," Slink said impatiently. "It's over by the Incubator. I'm sure they'll give you a ride if you want to go and take a look-see."

Edward dropped to his hands and knees and scurried into the opening. Slink ducked in after him and pulled the doors closed behind them. They waited silently while the sound of engines grew louder and then faded away. When they were sure the Jamooks had gone, the two began to move down the dimly lit tunnel.

The Gnome could walk hunched over, but Edward had to crawl. The floor of the tunnel was littered with trash, and it was rough on his knees, but in a short while the passage opened, and the boy could Groucho Walk. In another 10 yards, they turned a bend, and the tunnel ended in a narrow valley set deep within hills of refuse.

"Maybe we should just stay here until the Jamooks are gone and then go back to that portal we just left," Edward said. "If they remove the dead Jamook we might be able to get the cart out of the way."

"Jamooks aren't smart, but they're stubborn. They never quit. They'll watch that portal and might even plant sensors as well."

With Slink in the lead the two worked their way around and over mounds of broken appliances, twisted furniture, and rusted clothing racks hung with molded garments. At times they came out on what Slink referred to as Mook Trails. These were passageways through the debris that were wide enough for a Mookmobile to travel on. They didn't stay long on these Mook Trails but quickly climbed back up and over a mound of trash or ducked into a tunnel. Some of the tunnels were rather long and twisted, and Edward soon lost all sense of direction.

At one point a particularly difficult tunnel opened out into a valley set deep among mountains of junk that were higher than any he had seen during his short stay in STUFF-4-LESS. Slink chose a path, and they started up and out of the valley. They went on for the better part of an hour, all the while working higher and higher up into the trash hills and further and further from the portal back to BUY-N-BULK. High above the floor they had to cross a precarious hanging bridge made of two step ladders tied together and secured with extension cords.

"I don't see Jamooks making it across this bridge," Edward said while being very careful not to look down.

"The Jamooks can't get to us up here. Their motorized shopping carts aren't fit for any off-road action," Slink said as they picked their way around a landslide of busted shopping baskets. It was slow going because the sharp ends of wires jutted out at every angle. "They can spot us with drones if we aren't careful, but there's not much they can do about it."

"Drones?" Edward asked as he tried to free his pant leg from a wire.

"Remote control helicopters, hovercraft, planes; stuff like that," the Gnome answered. "Don't you have such things in BUY-N-BULK?"

Edward ripped his pant leg free and almost lost his balance in the process. "Yes, we do, but they're mostly toys we play with."

"Nobody plays for fun in STUFF-4-LESS anymore." Slink said as he sadly shook his head, "Over here we play for keeps."

They were picking their way along a particularly steep and narrow part of the trail near the top of one of the rubbish mountains when Slink suddenly grabbed Edward by the arm. "Hold still," the Gnome said.

Edward froze in his tracks. The trail, cut into the mountain of trash, was only slightly wider than his feet. The boy did not know why Slink told him to stop but as he stood there, he felt his heart racing and perspiration broke out on his forehead. He tried to get control of himself by taking deep breaths, at least as deep as he could without moving his chest. He closed his eyes and then, opening them again, looked out over the landscape below.

The ceiling was still far above them and the enclosed area stretched out seemingly forever. In places, the heaps of collapsed shelving and discarded merchandise were as high or higher than the one they were on. Some of the heaps were covered with vegetation, a jungle of house plants on steroids. These plants were constantly watered by a drizzle falling from cracked sprinkler heads mounted beneath the roof trusses far overhead. Some rubbish mountains smoldered from within like volcanoes, and a blueish-brown smoke found its way up from the top of these peaks and out through the roof by way of broken skylights. Shafts of sunlight illuminated the hazy atmosphere. Beyond the hills the landscape opened into plains across which whirlwinds of plastic shopping bags swirled. Beyond the plains were more hills. This pattern was repeated in every direction until lost to the curvature of the earth.

Most of what he saw was a landscape of wreckage, but in places the store was somewhat in order. In these small areas the shelves were vertical and at least partially stocked; and the aisles, while cluttered, were passable. The expanse was great and the air hazy, but he could see Jamooks cruising up and down these ordered aisles loading the baskets on their shopping carts. Gnomes were driving American Flyer wagons pulled by pink flamingos. The wagons were piled high with groceries, and the Gnomes were stocking the shelves.

Edward was just about to ask why they were stopped when a remotely controlled model helicopter sailed around the slope of the heap. Beneath the chopper a small black box was fastened with silver-gray duct tape.

"Very still," the Gnome said out of the corner of his mouth, "If we don't move, the Viper can't see us against all this trash."

The helicopter passed in a slow and jerky motion. Edward could see the red beam from a laser sight shining down from the front of the black box. He stiffened even more and, when he did so, he could feel some of the trash beneath his right foot begin to shift. An empty, store-brand, cola can worked loose from the pile and bounced, end over end, down the hillside. The copter stopped in flight and began to slowly turn in Edward's direction. He could see the red dot from the laser playing across the landscape and getting closer and closer to his position.

Slink spoke out the side of his mouth like a second-rate ventriloquist. "That's a Viper. If it spots us, the Hogs will come."

The two cut their eyes hard to the right to watch as the chopper continued its slow turn, and the red dot drew closer to their position.

CHAPTER 6

SNAP, CRINKLE, POP! The red laser dot was just inches away from the side of Edward's face when a section of the trash mountain across the valley broke loose. The cascading debris triggered a landslide that blocked the roadway far below. The Viper pivoted quickly, dropped ten feet, recovered, and darted across to the scene of the slide. Slink pulled Edward by the hand, and the two of them scurried to the top of the mountain and ducked behind the wheels of an upturned bicycle.

"Cleanup in Sector 2733," The loudspeaker rasped.

"How are pigs going to get way up here?" Edward asked.

"Not pigs, Hogs."

"But aren't pigs and hogs pretty much the same thing?"

"Hide and watch," Slink said as they looked out though the spokes.

"Is this adequate cover?" Edward plucked one of the spokes.

Those scout drones' sensors are primitive. They work off motion detectors and silhouette recognition. These metal bike wheel spokes will break up our silhouette, throws their radar off. A steady noise - vacuum cleaner, hair dryer, blender - will give them fits as well. Hogs can't see at all, they rely on the Vipers for direction." Slink said.

"How did you learn all this?"

"Trial and error. We lost a lot of Free Gnomes to gain this information."

"Who controls them, the Hogs and Vipers?" Edward asked.

"Fearon does. From his Command Center."

Across the narrow but very deep valley the Viper drone worked its way up and down in front of the trash hill targeting it with its laser pointer. In a matter of minutes, two larger helicopter drones appeared. Suspended between them by bungee cords was a crude bomb fashioned from a rubber yoga ball bristling with shotgun shells.

"Those are the Hogs," Slink said.

The two Hogs, yoked together by the bomb, pulled against each other and spun in circles like a South American bola. They overshot the top of the mound the Viper was pinpointing and dropped their payload on the far side. There was a large blast and shotgun pellets intermixed with chunks of debris shot up like a corona above the mound.

The two hogs, free from their burden and riddled with shot, took off in irregular trajectories. One of them darted right toward Slink and Edward's vantage point but, at the last second, veered off and flew into the open door of a front-loading washing machine embedded in the hillside just below them. The remaining Hog, flying erratically, took off in the direction from which it came. The viper followed behind targeting the Hog with the red dot.

"They don't seem to be very effective," Edward said.

"No, not in the least," Slink said as he shifted his position to a more comfortable seat. "From time to time a Free Gnome gets careless or a Hog gets lucky but, for the most part they just provide comic relief."

Edward started to get up, but the Gnome pulled him back down. "Wait for the road crew," he said. "They can't see us up here, their eyesight's too poor, but they are fun to watch.

In time, two Jamooks labored up the trail driving Mookmobiles with snow shovels mounted on the front. They worked back and forth on the trash slide below, banging into one another, growling, and pushing trash around in a very unproductive manner. Eventually they got most of it out of the trail.

After the road crew was gone Edward stood up and surveyed the landscape. "You really do live in the store, don't you?"

"Beautiful, isn't?" Slink beamed with pride. "Now, nobody's saying there's not a few spots that are a little rundown and in need of improvement but wait till you see Topside."

Edward noticed, for the first time, that the inverted bicycle they were hiding behind was fastened securely to the top of a particle board office desk which was, in turn, buried firmly in the mountain top. The chain on the bicycle did not run to the rear wheels as was customary but was very long and ran upward instead. The boy had been so focused on the action in the valley that he had not looked up. The chain ran from the front sprocket up to and through a platform that was woven among the trusses which were supporting the roof. This main platform was, in turn, connected to other platforms by means of heat and air ducts as well as hanging bridges.

Slink rolled up his sleeves and began to turn the pedal on his side of the bike. He nodded for Edward to do the same with the other pedal, and the boy joined in the task. There was much squeaking and grinding of metal, and an aluminum extension ladder began to lower down through a cutout in the bottom of the platform above. When the ladder was fully extended, Slink began to climb up toward the platform, and Edward followed.

When they reached the top, Slink spread his hands in an all-inclusive fashion. "This is Topside," he said, "home of the Free Gnomes."

Edward looked around. It was not at all what he had been led to expect but given the condition of the parts of STUFF-4-LESS he had already seen, that was not a big surprise. The space was cramped, and he could only move around by ducking under cables, conduit and ducts. There was a second inverted bicycle that Edward assumed was used, like the one below, to crank the ladder up and down. A beer cooler served as a table. There was a piece of a candle on a saucer atop the cooler and a chair fashioned from a plastic laundry detergent tub next to it. Dresser drawers, with no dresser, were stacked in one corner. Clothes hung out over their edges. Against one wall was a canvas cot with a thin pillow, thinner blanket, and no mattress.

A portrait hung on the wall above the cot. It was a likeness of Slink himself and was skillfully executed even though it seemed to be painted with dried mustard, Ketchup, and coffee grounds smeared on a pillowcase which was stretched over cardboard. The painting was signed "CLINK". A hammock was suspended in front of the window on the opposite wall. All the windows were small and draped on the outside with volleyball nets.

"Let's eat, I'm so hungry my belly button is starting to eat my belt buckle," Slink said as he put the plastic sack he had been carrying down on the drink cooler and sat on the detergent tub.

Edward looked around but could find nothing else that even remotely resembled a chair among the sparse furnishings.

"Sorry," Slink said. "Wherever are my manners? You need a place to sit, don't you? I guess I haven't had many visitors up here lately." He retrieved a blue plastic scrub bucket from beneath the cot, inverted it, and invited Edward to sit.

Slink divided up the cupcakes and cheese sticks. He popped open the cans of cola and slid one over in front of Edward. The Gnome held up the two bags of chips extending first one and then the other toward Edward like pistons. Edward pointed to the bag of regular chips, and Slink tossed it over to him. The cheese sticks were a bit slimy, the cupcakes stale, the cola warm, and the chips had suffered greatly on the journey; but Edward was hungry, and hunger trumps all.

When they had finished eating, Slink turned and threw his empty soda can out the window. Edward followed suit. The cans hit the volleyball nets and dropped into the trash below. Edward could now see that the volleyball nets were hung a few feet out from the windows. "What's the story with the nets?" He asked.

"The remotes haven't found this place yet. Viper cameras are designed to look around and down but not up," Slink explained. "I guess it's just a matter of time before they find Topside, but when they do, the nets will keep them from getting in here."

It was growing dark outside, and Edward could see the small, organized areas of STUFF-4-LESS beginning to light up. The overhead lighting throughout the vast store remained dark, but emergency lighting gave the whole place an eerie glow. With all the adventure, he realized that he had not thought about getting back to BUY-N-BULK in quite some time. "Where is the other portal?" he asked.

"What portal is that?" The Gnome asked as he began to work the pedals on the bicycle to raise the ladder.

"The other portal you told me about; the one that will get me back to BUY-N-BULK and back to my family," the boy said as he joined the Gnome in his labor.

The aluminum ladder inched higher and higher until it bumped against the metal roof. "Oh, right, that other portal," Slink said. "We'll make our way over there first thing in the morning. Right now, we should get some sleep. You take the cot; I'll sleep in the hammock by the window where I can keep an eye out."

Edward lay down on the cot and tried to get comfortable as best he could. "There's a flashlight under your pillow," Slink said. "Most nights they cut the emergency lights, and it gets pretty dark, but don't use it unless you have to; batteries are hard to come by."

It took Edward a long time to get to sleep but once he did, he slept hard. When he awoke it was still night and dark. Edward had never experienced such total darkness. He thought he saw something move, a figure, black on black, over by the table. He held his breath and fumbled for the flashlight. The shape by the table made a sudden move with its arm and a ball of fire burst into its hand.

CHAPTER 7

Slink held the match and rolled it over in his fingers until it was burning well and then lit the candle on the table. "It will be daylight soon, and we'll need to find some breakfast," he said.

"Perhaps we can get breakfast on our way to the portal," Edward suggested as he sat up and pulled on one of his shoes.

"We can't go back to the portal, at least not anytime soon." Slink inverted the empty potato chip bag above his mouth and tried to shake out the last few crumbs. "I thought I explained all that to you yesterday."

"I'm not talking about that portal, the one I came through," Edward said as he poked under the cot looking for his second shoe. "I'm talking about the other portal, the one you told me about yesterday. You remember? You said it would take a while to get there. I'm sure we'll find something worth eating along the way."

"Well, kid, about that other portal," Slink said as he licked the last bit of icing from the top of the cupcake box. "I may have exaggerated just a little bit on that one. In fact, I may have exaggerated a good deal. There is no other portal, at least not one I'm aware of."

Edward Eliot Emmons stopped tying his shoes and looked at the Gnome. "What do you mean?"

The Gnome extended his arms out to the sides with the palms up. "I had to get you out of that cooler. There was no time to waste. If that second Jamook cornered us in there we would have been history or, more precisely, lunch. Let's just say, the Jamook palate has no known limits."

At first Edward could think of nothing to say, and then the words came out and would not stop. "Are you telling me there is no other portal? Everything you said yesterday, it was all just a story? A story you made up on the spot?

"And, while we're on the subject of false information, this place is far from the fun-filled theme park you reported it to be. As far as I can tell, it's a land composed almost entirely of rubbish. It's a giant landfill infested with flying drones that drop bombs and horrid creatures riding in supercharged shopping carts and stuffing their mouths the whole while with all manner of junk food... and did I mention the rubbish? This place, this land of the Free Gnomes, is perfectly dreadful; and I'm stuck here with no way back home. Is that what you're telling me?"

Slink walked over to the window and looked out. The skylights were beginning to appear in the form of faint rectangles suspended in the air.

"And where are the rest of the Gnomes?" Edward continued with his rant, "This marvelous race of Free Gnomes that you told me all about. As far as I can see, you're the only one."

Slink hung his head by way of answer.

"There aren't any other Free Gnomes, are there?" The boy said in a softer voice.

"No, there aren't. At least none that are free," Slink said. "I'm the last."

"I'm sorry," Edward said. "I didn't know.

Slink walked over and sat down on the bed next to Edward. "All the other Gnomes have been enslaved. You saw them yesterday, down below, driving the flamingo wagons and stocking the shelves for the Fearonjamooks. Look, I don't know if there are more gateways to the other side or not. It took us a long time just to find the one."

"So that was your first trip to the portal?" Edward asked.

The light outside had grown stronger, and Slink got up and blew out the candle on the table. "That may well have been the first trip anyone ever made to any portal. Until now such things as portals and a BUY-N-BULK populated by humans existed only in legend. My hope was to find the gateway, if there was such a thing, and pass through it to recruit some help. I plan to free the Gnomes and rid this land of evil. I may not succeed, but I must try, there's nothing else I can do."

"You said 'us'."

"What do you mean?"

"You said it took 'us' a long time to the find the portal," the boy said as he finished tying his shoes.

"I have a friend that has been working with me."

"Is he a Gnome?"

"No," Slink replied. "He's a she, and she's not a Gnome. But she's the only one in this place I can trust."

"I'll help you too," Edward Eliot Emmons volunteered, and then quickly regretted his words. His father had often warned him about speaking before he thought completely through the state of affairs. "Would Jamooks really eat a human?"

"No, I doubt a Jamook would eat a human. I should think human is an acquired taste, and Jamooks wouldn't have much chance to acquire such a taste here in STUFF-4-LESS where there are no humans. Besides, they favor a diet rich in processed, prepackaged foods that are high in salt, fat, and cholesterol," the Gnome said as he began to crank the ladder back down. "All that talk about salt, fat and cholesterol has made me even more hungry.

"Still, this could be very dangerous," Slink said as the ladder hit bottom." It might be best to try and find a way to get you back to BUY-N-BULK."

"Yes, that plan sounds very good as well," Edward said with great relief. "But how will we manage that without access to a portal?"

Slink stepped out onto the ladder and started down. "We can start by visiting my friend. She's the one who really found the first portal, and if she can find one, she might be able to find more."

Edward was just about to step out onto the ladder when Slink reversed course and scurried back up through the hole. The platform shook with an explosion, and a spray of pellets burst up through the opening. Slink dropped and rolled clear from the shot. The aluminum ladder twisted sideways, hung there momentarily, and then dropped down out of sight. Edward could hear the ladder rattle amongst the debris below. And then all was quiet, deadly quiet. Smoke came up through the opening, and the smell of gun powder hung heavy in the air

CHAPTER 8

"There's a bunch of them, thick as ticks. They've found Topside. Vipers and Hogs everywhere." Slink said as he jumped to his feet and leaped onto the cot.

Edward did not know why the Gnome had jumped up onto the cot, but he jumped up on the cot as well. Another explosion shook the floor, and a Viper tangled in the volleyball net outside the window. The Viper and the net fell away. "How did they find us?"

"I don't know but found we are," Slink said as he pulled aside the pillowcase portrait revealing a round, dark opening behind it. Edward recognized it as a large heat and air duct. The Gnome pushed the boy in and quickly followed. "In all haste," Slink advised.

They had made it just a few yards down the tunnel when there was another loud explosion. Both the boy and Gnome looked back. What they could see of Topside fell from view.

There was not enough room for Edward to travel in any manner other than in a hands and knees crawl. Slink clomped along at the boy's heels. "I thought we'd be safe in Topside. The sensor mounts on Viper bellies don't allow them to look up," Slink said.

In about ten yards they reached a point where the round duct connected with a square box that was somewhat roomier. In the middle of the floor of the box was a vent and square beams of light streamed upward through the grill. Edward scurried out onto the vent, and the vent gave way. He could see the metal grill tumbling toward the junk heap below and felt himself falling after it. He closed his eyes, expecting the worst and not wanting to see what was to happen next. At the last possible second, he was pulled up short. The boy dangled upside down from the vent hole, his coat hung down from his arms like a sail on an inverted boat. He looked up to see Slink with a two-handed death grip on his ankle.

Back in the direction of topside, or in the direction where topside once was, Edward could see Vipers and Hogs buzzing around like a swarm of angry bees. They were focused on the chunks of debris that were still falling from the rafters. "Some of the Vipers have sensors on their roofs and some Hogs have rockets," he yelled up to Slink.

"Took them long enough to figure that one out," Slink said. "Hang on, if I pull you up slowly, they may not see us."

Edward looked back down in the direction of the drones and, as he did, their red laser lights played over his jacket which was flapping in the air. "Too late," he said, "Here they come."

"Your pricer," Slink said as he held on with all his might.

"My what?"

"The pricer you took from the Jamook in the cooler. Remember, you put it in your jacket pocket," the Gnome said. "Now might be a good time to learn to use it."

Edward fumbled the weapon loose from his jacket pocket, aimed it in the direction of the swarm of drones, and fired. The bright green laser beam scored a direct hit on one of the Hogs. The bomb the large drone was carrying swung wildly from the end of its bungee cord. The damaged drone spun out of control, hurling the bomb into the rotor of a passing Viper. The explosion sent buckshot flying. Airborne pellets started a chain reaction which, in turn, nearly cleared the skies of drones. Slink pulled Edward up through the hole as shot rattled around them.

"Well done my young friend," Slink said as they worked their way around the gaping vent hole and started once again down the tunnel of duct work. "Two more sections and then make a right. Straight on from there, and mind the vent covers. We can't afford to lose a soldier of your caliber."

The boy wasn't sure if it was a lucky shot or not. Aside from shooting one stationary milk container back in the cooler, he had no other experience with a pricer. Still, who was to say he was not simply a natural with the weapon. Edward Eliot Emmons beamed with pride as he stuck the weapon back in his jacket pocket.

He counted two more sections, each one delineated by a box with a vent in the floor. He turned to the right as instructed and saw before him a seemingly endless passageway of duct work. At regular intervals light filtered up through the vents in the floor. The pattern went on forever, disappearing finally in the gloom. Edward did another five sections and then stopped to rest in one of the vent boxes, being careful not to sit on the grating.

Slink joined him and sat against the opposite wall. "Time for a little breather," he said as he lifted the grate up out of the vent hole and looked down trying to get his bearings.

The two of them rested and surveyed the forlorn landscape. "This used to be a wonderful place, everything I said it was and more. Gnomes could come and go as they pleased, and pink flamingos were pets and not beasts of burden. As for Jamooks, well, the Jamooks were always annoying but docile and easily controlled. They did menial work like stocking shelves and mopping floors. Their carts were battery-powered, and they needed Gnomes to recharge them. Battery-powered carts have very big batteries and very little power. Put a broom handle on the floor in front of one, and it would stop it deader than Disco."

"Disco?" Edward asked.

"It was music. Well, sort of music. About as sincere as Cool-Whip. It showed up around the same time as Fearon. Some say it came over from BUY-IN-BULK. Some say he did too. Anyway, back in the days of the battery powered rides we could corral a whole herd of Jamooks with 100 foot of garden hose. Now they have Mookmobiles, gas powered and turbocharged. Nothing stands in the way of a Fearonjamook."

"What happened to make them change and become Fearonjamooks?" Edward asked.

"What happened? Fearon the Feared happened. That's what happened," Slink said as he dropped the grate back in place over the hole. "Let's talk about something else."

"Tell me about your friend. You said she was not a Gnome."

"No, she's a robot," Slink said as he got up and climbed into the duct opening on the opposite side from which they had come. "Her name is Adele, and she lives in Electronics. It's about seven sections down the line from here."

"I can't wait to meet her," Edward said as he followed the Gnome. "I'm sure she'll be able to help us."

Slink stopped in his tracks and turned back to Edward. "Listen Edward, I don't know if you've had a lot of experience with women. You might be a little young for such things, but they're somewhat different from us. For one thing, they can be mighty sensitive about their looks. You see, Adele is a unique design, and, well, her looks are ... "

"Her looks are very...creative?" Edward chimed in.

"Creative," Slink said as they started once again on their journey. "Yes, creative, that's it exactly. Edward, my boy, I suspect you'll do very well with women."

After crossing seven sections they reached a junction box that was larger and more brightly lit than the others. One of the outgoing sections of duct had broken loose and was hanging down like a long chute. Light poured in through the broken joint at the top.

"In you go," Slink said.

Edward leaned over and looked down the long tube but could see nothing but darkness. "I'm not sure this is such a good idea."

"Feet first is my advice," Slink said.

Edward got down and, scooting on his backside, worked his feet into the opening. When he sat poised on the lip of the chute, he turned his head back to look at Slink. "I just don't know if I'm ready for this. Is it safe?"

"Safe enough," Slink said. "Besides, there isn't another way down."

"Maybe we should look around just to be sure."

Slink pushed Edward into the tunnel. "Keep your hands folded across your chest!" The Gnome shouted after the rapidly disappearing boy.

Edward hugged himself tightly and tried not to scream. He sped down the tube and around several bends. The only light was sparks of static electricity set off by his clothing. He finally shot out into a carefully placed shopping basket. His momentum propelled the basket forward and a lid, fashioned from a wire oven shelf, snapped down and locked in place. As the basket rolled forward it pulled a second shopping cart into position.

Slink shot out of the vent and landed in the second basket whose lid also locked in place.

The second basket, the one containing the Gnome, rolled across the floor and bumped into the cart that held Edward. The traps were well made, and while the two friends faced each other, they were each packed tightly in their own basket. There was little room to maneuver.

"Well, I must admit, this is a bit of a surprise," Slink said.

Edward was about to reply when a shadow fell over the two shopping carts.

CHAPTER 9

The shadow grew closer and loomed over the two carts. Edward shifted his position and looked up as best he could. What he saw, perched on top of a battered chest freezer, was a most amazing creature. Perhaps creature wasn't the right word to use. A creature is usually something that's alive. What Edward was looking at was more a machine than an animal.

The body of this machine was made up of a computer tower fastened firmly down into a pink, electric convertible. It was the kind of car that was meant for a large doll or a small child. There were arms, many of them. One was made from a gripper, the kind that old people use to pick things up off the floor and short people use to get things down from the top shelf. Another was a yellow scoop arm from a toy steam shovel. These arms, and several others, were mounted in various locations around the body of the car. The most striking part of this machine was the boxy, old, computer monitor that was fastened on top of the tower. Two small cameras extended from either side of this monitor and a microphone the size of a softball stuck up from the top. Crowning the microphone, fastened at an angle, was a plastic sunflower the size of a dinner plate. A large car battery, mounted on a skateboard, trailed along behind.

The monitor on top of the machine swiveled and the cameras tilted down to face the boy trapped in the baskets. Edward twisted up, as best he could, to look at the monitor. Question marks bounced around the display like an old-time screen saver.

"How are you doing, Adele?" Slink said. "You wouldn't have something to eat around here, would you?"

The robot's monitor spun around to face Slink. A picture of a cartoon character with steam coming out of its ears flashed on the screen.

"She's mad," Slink whispered to Edward.

"I guessed as much," Edward said.

Adele spun around and motored down a plastic playground slide. When she reached the bottom she glared at Slink, at least as much as a construction without an actual face can glare.

"Now might be an excellent opportunity to try some of your boyish charm," Slink whispered.

"That's a lovely, uh, ensemble you have there. Did you make it yourself?" Edward asked.

Adele's monitor spun around and faced him. A big, cheesy grin lit up the boy's face. A grin that was clearly part of a toothpaste ad filled the robot's display. One of her arms, a drop hook from an arcade game, plucked open the latch on the top of the basket. Edward flipped the lid back, sat up and began to work the feeling back into his arms and legs.

"Yeah, that's right, lovely insoluble, onsolvable ... what he said," Slink offered up.

Without turning her monitor to look in his direction, Adele shot out another one of her arms, one that looked to be an extension tube with a gripper on the end for changing light bulbs. The bulb gripper took hold of Slink's basket and shook it violently. The helpless Gnome was compressed into the far corner of his cage.

The robot let go of the basket and then, almost as an afterthought, released the latch that held the top in place.

Slink sat up and tried to pull himself together. "Listen Adele ..." he started to say, but the robot's monitor spun in his direction flashing a video of an oncoming steam engine moving at a high rate of speed. Billows of smoke poured from its stack.

Slink leaned back against the far side of the shopping basket, nearly tipping it over. The robot righted it with another one of her arms.

"I know I haven't been here in a while," Slink said.

Calendar pages ran backwards across Adele's screen and then stopped. A red circle appeared around one of the dates. There was a clicking and a whirring, and a printed page protruded out of a slot in the robot's car. She pulled the page free and handed it to Slink.

"OK, it's been more than a while," Slink said as he glanced down at the print-out, "But I found it, I found the portal."

Adele's monitor spun 360 degrees, and exclamations points bounced across her screen followed by an explosion of star bursts. One of her gripper arms reached out and pinched Slink's cheek.

"My friend Edward here came through it. He came through from BUY-N-BULK. I can't wait to tell you all about it" Slink said. "Perhaps we can do it over some lunch. You see, we had to leave Topside in a bit of a hurry and didn't have much time for breakfast."

The star bursts on Adele's monitor were replaced by a picture of a 1950s, TV mother. The woman was wearing an apron with frills and posed in a 1950's TV kitchen.

"That would be right nice," Slink said as he climbed down out of the basket. "Come on Edward, Adele is going to make us something to eat."

Adele's monitor swiveled to face the boy as he jumped down out of his shopping cart as well. A series of pictures of mother animals with their babies and dogs with big eyes replaced one another on the screen. Adele shot out two gripper arms and pinched both of Edward's cheeks.

"I think she's taken a liking to you," Slink said as the two fell in behind the robot.

Edward could see that they were in a valley surrounded by rubbish hills. Protruding from the top of these hills, at regular intervals, were metal shepherd's crooks with bug zappers hanging down. Next to each one was an oversized drinking bird, about four feet tall.

"Those bug zappers are the best at jamming Viper's radar and their guidance system as well," Slink explained. "The drones can't get past them without spinning out of control. The drinking birds charge batteries that provide power for the zappers at night or in case Fearon cuts the main power source. Without surveillance, Fearon and his Jamooks have no idea what's here in Adele's compound. But you can bet the farm, they want to know."

The three worked themselves through a maze of shelves that were placed close together with just enough room between them for Adele to move easily. "All these shelves are bolted down," Slink explained. "The aisles are too narrow for Jamooks to maneuver in even if there's a security breach."

At one point the shelving maze opened into a larger clear space with the feel of a workshop. One side featured a project bench, well-lit by goose-neck lamps and backed with a section of pegboard hung with tools. An outline was drawn around each tool and each tool was hung precisely in its proper space.

"Maybe you could show Edward how one of your Weasels works," Slink said to Adele.

The robot flashed another big smile at Edward. On the workbench was a small tin box that was painted on all sides with circus designs. Adele picked up a CD player, hit the on button, and "Pop Goes the Weasel" began to play. Edward stepped forward to get a better look at the box, but Slink firmly pulled him back. When the song reached its climax the "Pop" caused the box to fly open and send a spray of small, sharp nails across the surface of the workbench and a few out onto the floor.

Edward was not sure exactly what to think of the demonstration. "That was very entertaining," he said.

Without further explanation, Adele started down one of the aisles that led away from the work room. Slink and Edward followed. In a short while Adele turned right, and the two travelers turned also. In front of them was a tunnel opening. It was wider than the other passageways in Adele's compound, as wide as a Mook trail. They entered the tunnel, which was a short one, and stopped just short of the far end.

There was a Mook trail there that seemed to lead right into the tunnel and just turning onto that trail, just a few yards away was a Mookmobile. It was traveling at a high rate of speed and a very fierce looking Jamook wearing a bedpan for a helmet was at the helm. The creature was armed with a pickax in one scabbard and a sledgehammer in the other. The engine of its motorized shopping cart was revved up and a plume of blue-black smoke billowed out behind.

CHAPTER 10

The Jamook, despite its high rate of speed, was eating handfuls of cat food from a ten-pound bag in its basket on the front of his vehicle and washing them down with a box of instant mashed potatoes. So intent was the creature on its meal that it did not seem to see the three intruders who were directly in its path.

Edward put his hands over his eyes, being careful to spread his fingers enough to see clearly and waited for the crash. But the crash never happened. Just before the Jamook ran them down, it spun the wheel on its cart and turned hard left down a Mook Trail that Edward had not noticed. He leaned forward to see where the Jamook had gone and, when he did so, conked his head on a crystal-clear pane of glass.

Slink laughed with delight. "It's a window from out of the display case in the Deli Department. It's got a special coating on it that Adele invented. Makes it as clear as air."

Edward put his face as close to the glass as he could, or at least as close to where he thought it was. He could just make out a slight ripple in the air. As he reached out to touch the glass, the Jamook shot back in front of the opening and looked right at him, only inches away. Edward would have fallen over on the seat of his pants if Adele had not caught him with one of her arms.

"The coating also makes it a one-way mirror," Slink said in a soft voice. "That creature can't see us at all what with the darkness of the tunnel behind where we are."

The Jamook looked in the mirror and wiped powdered potatoes from the side of its face. The creature then removed its bedpan hat and began to primp the long greasy braids of its hair.

"Jamooks are extremely vain," Slink said. "Get down and look up under the cart."

As instructed, Edward got down on his hands and knees and looked under the creature's motorized shopping cart. In order to be able to see itself in the mirror the Jamook had parked on a rubber pad of some sort. A small door opened in the center of the pad and out of the opening came a mechanical arm holding a brightly painted Weasel. The arm extended to within half an inch of the bottom of the cart, and the Weasel leaped up and attached itself firmly to the undercarriage. "A magnet?" Edward asked as the mechanical arm quickly withdrew.

"That's right," Slink said. "Adele has been tagging Mookmobiles with Weasels for quite some time now. It's hard to say how many there are out there, but she's tagged a whole lot of them."

"So, when the Weasels go off, the nails will stick in the tires; and the tires will go flat," Edward said.

"Right again, my boy," Slink said. "A Jamook without wheels is nearly useless, a sitting duck for a Free Gnome platoon. The only problem is that the music has to be either very loud or fairly close to the Weasel to make it pop."

"Yes," Edward said. "That and the fact that we don't have a Free Gnome platoon on hand."

"What say we go eat now?' Slink said, changing the subject. "That Jamook has flung a craving on me. I believe I'm hungry enough to eat cat food if there aren't any better choices."

They started back along the narrower trails and deeper into Adele's compound. The shelves they passed were neatly stocked with electronics, car parts, mechanical toys and tools. The maze opened to a central space that was roomy and well-organized. Edward could tell this was Adele's kitchen. One wide shelf held a microwave, toaster oven and an electric skillet. Above the workspace the shelves were stocked with all manner of kitchen gadgets and small appliances. At one end of the kitchen was an alcove that served as a pantry. The robot motored into the pantry and came back out with half a dozen cans of food which she seemed to have picked at random.

Adele set to work with all her arms moving at once and began to prepare a meal in the electric skillet.

In the middle of the space was a table made of a door lying atop two folding aluminum saw horses. At one end was a highchair. Slink, making himself at home, climbed up into the highchair. There was no other seat.

Edward looked around, but the only thing he could find that would serve as a chair was a large, metallic blue, exercise ball. He rolled it up to the table and tried, as best he could, to make himself comfortable. Painted on the table in front of him was an outsized stick figure silhouette of a man and the word MEN.

Adele was opening cans with one arm, chopping up ingredients with another, and stirring the contents of the skillet with a third. She swiveled her monitor 180 degrees and faced Slink. Pictures of doors and windows interspersed with large colorful question marks ran across the screen.

"I guess, you want to hear all about the portal?" Slink said as he leaned back in his chair and put his feet up on the table.

Dramatic pictures of lightning strikes and much less dramatic pictures of shoes flashed across the robot's screen.

Slink hurriedly put his feet back down on the floor. "Sorry about that. Now, where was I? Oh yeah, the portal."

Adele rotated one of her cameras to the rear so she could cook and listen at the same time. Slink settled in and began his story. "Well, you know how we narrowed it down to about half a dozen sections?"

The robot flashed question marks and exclamation points as she took a folder down from a top shelf and placed it on the table in front of the boy.

"Okay, okay it was mostly you who did the narrowing." Slink conceded.

Edward picked up the folder. The cover was pink and had a picture of kittens playing with a ball of yarn.

Inside were pages of lined composition paper covered with numbers, arrows and hand drawn maps. "How did you know to even look for it, the portal I mean?" he asked.

"Every Free Gnome knows stories of BUY-N-BULK, but mostly we just think of them as myth. It was the place that our parents told us we would have to go if we didn't eat our vegetables. And yet, from time to time, artifacts would show up here in STUFF-4-LESS that didn't have any explanation. Things that must have come from somewhere else. Adele's mother board is an example,"

Adele's monitor beamed a prideful smile.

Slink went on, "If there was a BUY-N-BULK, and stuff from there was getting over here, then there had to be some kind of a connection, a portal. We thought if we could find it and get to BUY-N-BULK, as primitive as it might be over there, we could get some help."

Edward flipped through the pages, but the only part he could understand was the pink kitten cover.

"Anyway," Slink continued with his narrative. "I've been working over there in section 1403 for more than a week now. We, err, Adele said that if the portal was in 1403 at all, it would be somewhere between Baby Supplies and Soft Drinks. It was slow going because there's a major Mook Trail comes up out of Shoes and turns down right in front of Diapers. A lot of open territory there where they cut way back on the Crafts Department, a good chance I'd be exposed. I had to build tunnels to get around unnoticed and work mostly at night. I was living off diet drinks and cans of Simulac. I'm here to tell you, that stuff gets old in a hurry."

"Simulac? Isn't that what they feed babies?" Edward said as he tried to maintain his balance on the big blue ball. "My little brother, Clemens, used to drink that, and I always wondered what it tasted like."

"It tastes kind of sweet at first, sickly sweet," Slink said as he put his feet back up on the table. "But taste isn't the worst part of it. The worst part is the texture. It's slimy, and it plays havoc with your digestive track. I had to mix it half-in-two with edible glue from what was left of the Crafts Department just to get ..."

Adele's shot out one of her grippers and lifted Slink's feet off the table. The pictures of doors, windows, and question marks once again played across her screen.

"Right, as I was saying, I'd pretty much worked over the whole quadrant and was about to quit when I realized I missed a section. It was just a small area. I was going to forget about it and go because I figured it was such a small area and way too dangerous being right on the edge of the Mook Trail like it was."

Adele swiveled her camera that was facing the table up to the shelves. The robot reached out one of her grippers and took down two plastic bowls. She swiveled her camera back to the table and put one bowl in front of Slink and one in front of Edward. Edward's had a picture of a teddy bear in the bottom of the bowl and two teddy bear ear handles extending from the rim. It was teddy bear brown.

"But I figured I'd come that far, I may as well see it through," Slink continued. "I started moving the debris, real careful like. I didn't want a landslide that would draw the drones and tip the Jamooks to my being there. I was expecting to find a blank wall, you know, what was left of the Dairy section that butts up against Soft Drinks. I had dug into the rubbish about three feet when I realized that the wall was there right enough, and it had a door in it." Slink pulled the pink folder over in front of himself, flipped it open to a page with an intricate map and placed his finger on the spot where he had found the hidden door.

Adele focused the camera she was not using for meal preparation down onto the map, produced a red marker, and put a large red X on the spot. She then swiveled the camera that was facing the folder back up to the shelves and tried to find two coffee mugs that weren't chipped, badly stained or full of nuts and bolts.

Edward took advantage of the robot's momentary inattention and swapped bowls with Slink. The quick movement caused the exercise ball he was sitting on to bounce and sway. As the robot rotated her camera back Edward looked down into his new bowl. At the bottom was a picture of a dog bone and the word FIDO.

"It took me a spell to dig a hole deep enough and wide enough to free the door," Slink continued with his tale. "I had to shore up sections so the whole hillside wouldn't come down on me. I had the Jamook patrols figured pretty well, but I didn't want to take any chances."

The robot stirred the concoction in the skillet with one arm and put the cups on the table with a second arm while opening a large jug of sports drink the color of antifreeze. with a third. She turned her camera back away from the table to look for spoons and Edward quickly swapped the bowls back again. The ball he was sitting on tilted forward and his head almost hit the table.

Adele spun around with the skillet and ladled a generous helping into the two bowls while handing each of her guests a spoon. Slink dug in, eating as fast as he could blow each spoonful cool. Edward righted himself and looked down at what he took to be stew. He picked up a little on the end of his spoon and sniffed it. "I recognize the corn, mini ravioli, pineapple bits and pinto beans but what gives the whole thing that greenish look?" he asked.

"That's creamed spinach," Slink said as he paused briefly. "And the meat is Spam. It's one of Adele's specialties. Say, could you pass the mustard?"

"Anyway," the Gnome said as he got back to his story, "when I got the door free, I should have filled in the passageway behind me with at least a curtain of trash. You know, so the Jamooks wouldn't see that somebody had been digging there. I understand that now, it's what I should have done, but I was really excited and all."

Even with the inconvenience of telling the tale Slink still managed to empty his bowl.

Edward tried to pick some of the corn out of the mixture and wipe the creamed spinach off. His exercise ball seat tilted dramatically to the right.

Slink gave the boy a troubled look but went on with the story. "When I got the door opened and stepped inside, I knew right away I was onto something. The shelves were neatly stacked, and the cooler was, well, cool. There were things on the shelves I didn't recognize. I knew the products well enough, and the national brands were the same, but the store brand was different. It wasn't Stuffer-Stuff brand like we have here, but Bulk-Buys.

"There was an identical door on the other end of the cooler, and I was in the process of trying to figure out how to get up to the handle of the second door and unlatch it when Edward came tumbling in."

Adele had just refilled his bowl, and the Gnome was beginning to tell the story of his first encounter with Edward when she rotated her microphone upward as if a sound had caught her attention. The boy could hear it now as well. A faint humming sound was coming from the sky, or what passed for the sky in this bizarre world, and it was growing louder and louder.

Edward looked up and saw a large, circular shape passing overhead in near silence. He realized, from the turquoise color and the seahorses designs around the edge, that what he was looking at was the bottom side of an inflatable kids wading pool. From the top rim of the pool, ropes extended upward, and inflatable Halloween lawn pumpkins floated above. He was watching intently, spellbound by the sight, when the evil grinning head of a Jamook leaned over the edge of the pool. Edward Eliot Emmons fell backward off his exercise ball.

CHAPTER 11

"Helium," Slink said as he grabbed Edward by the ankles and dragged him under the crude table.

"Helium?" Edward questioned as he peeked out.

"They must have gotten it over in Card and Party. There's tons of that stuff over there." Slink said as he pulled Edward back. "It's used to fill birthday balloons. They've filled that kiddy pool and those inflatable pumpkins with helium, and it's given them enough lift to clear the ramparts."

"Why didn't the defense system stop them?" the boy asked.

This time it was Slink who peeked out. "They're being propelled by box fans probably powered by car batteries, just like Adele. Too low-tech to be affected by the bug zappers." He still held his spoon in his hand and was using it as a pointer. "My guess is, that fellow is on a reconnaissance mission.

From their position under the table, they could see that Adele had backed into the recess of the pantry. Edward had not noticed it before, but the pantry looked like a fallout shelter of sorts. It was quite sturdy, formed by shelves and covered over with all manner of discarded items. On her screen, the robot was flashing a red palm like the ones on the WALK/DON'T WALK signs at street corners. Edward and Slink held their position.

The shadow of the pool passed over the table and began to move away. Both the Gnome and boy peeked out to see where it was going. The Jamook swiveled the box fan that propelled the pool, and the flying ship banked into a slow turn that would bring it back over their position. They could see the Jamook clearly now. The creature was holding a weed whacker with the safety guard removed and a large, table saw blade in place of the trimming strings. The Jamook pulled the cord and fired up the whacker.

Edward looked back at Adele. She was now flashing the universal WALK sign except the white stick figure man was wind-milling his legs in a frantic manner.

The Jamook was coming back overhead and revving up his weed whacker to a crescendo as he waved it menacingly over his head. Unfortunately, the beast was, at the same time, trying to dump an entire box of powdered donuts into its mouth. The creature's attention was divided, and as a result, he did a poor job of both tasks. The donuts bounced down his front, and the whacker's blade made short work of several of the ropes that secured the inflatable Halloween pumpkins to the wading pool.

Too late the Jamook recognized his mistake. As the severed pumpkins rose toward the ceiling, the pool began to tilt. The Jamook tried desperately to hold his position, but it was of no use. The pool tipped forward, and the huge creature fell downward toward the table pulling the pool behind him.

Slink reached up to the tabletop and tried to scoop one last spoonful of lunch from his bowl. Edward grabbed the Gnome by the back of his collar and pulled him across the opening toward the pantry. Slink abandoned his spoon but managed to grab one of the flying powdered donuts.

The boy and Slink reached the shelter and turned to watch the carnage. The Jamook, still trying to manage the weed whacker, crashed down, headfirst, onto the table. The makeshift table collapsed, and the weed whacker tore into the plastic kiddy pool releasing the helium. The Jamook rolled over onto the floor and lay motionless.

Slink pointed up into the air. Flying Jamooks seemed to be everywhere. "They must have launched an entire armada," his voice was very high and squeaky.

"Why are you talking that way?" Edward asked and then realized he too was squeaking.

"Helium," Slink squeaked and handed the donut to Edward who hadn't eaten any stew.

Edward ate the donut while the three watched from the relative safety of their position. The airborne Jamook assault continued. In the near distance one of the beasts dropped a series of shotgun shell infused football bombs which exploded in rapid succession. Most of the shock wave and flying steel pellets were absorbed by the surrounding shelves. But, as would be expected, or should have been expected, some of the pellets shot upward and shredded the bottom of the Jamook's flying pool. It went down beyond the horizon of rubbish, out of view of the pantry. There was a horrible crunching noise followed by quiet. Several helium inflated pumpkin heads, freed by the crash, floated into view and on up toward the ceiling. One of the floating pumpkins found its way through a broken skylight and continued up out of sight.

A flying Jamook spotted the three friends in the pantry and came around hard in their direction. The creature, while trying to fire up a small chainsaw, miscalculated his altitude and tore the bottom out of his pool on a jagged edge of a full-length mirror that stuck up from the top of a trash ridge. The Jamook lost his expression of triumph as he went down through the slash, juggling the saw as he fell. He landed hard.

Another Jamook, in need of a snack on his way to battle, lowered a rope with a treble hook on the end and tried to snag a 50 lb. bag of potatoes. He was lucky and snagged the sack on the first pass. Regrettably, the weight of spuds tipped the flying wading pool, and the Jamook slid off the back. They could not see where he fell, but judging by the thud, it was not an easy landing. The wading pool craft turned upside-down, and several football bombs tumbled out. Although not visible, the blasts sounded impressive. The pool went down, and more pumpkin heads drifted up.

Slink stepped out from the shelter of their hiding place and took a bite of his donut as he looked up in the air. "I believe we are winning this battle," he said. "I can see only two remaining Jamooks aloft."

Edward went outside as well and looked up. There was quite a collection of floating pumpkin heads gathering against the ceiling. At the same time, he spotted the two flying Jamooks, they spotted him. One of them was armed with a battery powered saber saw, the other with an oversize police taser made from a metal leaf rake and jumper cables. They maneuvered their flying swimming pools around and began to zero in on the boy and Slink. Each creature was determined to be the one to make the kill. They rammed their ships together, albeit in slow motion, and hurled food and unintelligible curses across the gap.

The Jamook with the saber saw took a swipe at the one with the leaf rake taser. He missed but managed to cut several of the helium filled pumpkins loose. The

Jamook with the lawn rake slid forward as his craft began to list. He jabbed out with his weapon and burned a jagged hole in the side of his opponent's kiddy pool. The airships came together, and their pumpkin ropes tangled. The two were losing altitude fast and heading right toward the entrance to the pantry. Slink and Edward dashed back into safety just as 600 pounds of Jamook smashed in behind them. Everything went dark.

CHAPTER 12

"Is everybody all right?" Slink asked. The pantry was sturdy but not very deep. They were held firmly in place by the deflated pool and the deflated pool was held in place by the weight of the two Jamooks.

"I'm good, but I can hardly move. Can you check on Adele? I think she's behind me," Edward said while turning his neck as far as it would go. "All I can see is that her monitor has gone dark, and I think her cameras are missing as well."

"She's dead in the water," Slink said. "Do you know anything about computers?"

"I have one at home," Edward offered.

"Do you know how to fix it?"

"The first thing to do is to find the ON/Off button and push it," Edward said as he tried to work his way around far enough to face the computer. "I don't think I'll be able to reach it."

"I might be able to get to it," Slink said as he tried to make room by wiggling his shoulders. "Tell me what to look for."

"It's a recessed button on the front of the tower," Edward explained. "Right about where your belly button would be."

"I'm a garden Gnome," Slink said. They were very cramped in the pantry, and he was getting a bit testy. "Did you ever hear of a garden Gnome with a belly button?"

"No, I haven't," Edward conceded. "But, then again, I never heard of a garden Gnome who ate mystery stew and asked for seconds."

"Point taken," Slink said as he freed one hand and waved it in the air.

"The button is on the front, a little more than halfway down, in the middle." Edward explained. "Push it in, and count to five."

Slink found the ON/OFF button on Adele's tower, pushed in, and held it. He counted to five and then let go. There was a whirring sound followed by a bit of disjointed music as her screen came to life. By the light of her monitor, they could see their predicament. One of the deflated Jamook kiddy pools had draped over the entrance to the pantry during the crash. A large form, one which they took to be the Jamook itself, was tight up against the pool on the outside. Slink found a fork on a shelf near his head and used it to poke hard at the Jamook through the plastic pool. There was no response. "I think this one is dead," he said.

Edward managed to free one hand as well and began to rearrange the canned goods on the shelf he was pressed against. Some he pushed to the right, some he pushed to the left, but mostly he pushed them off the back. In a short while he cleared a space big enough for him to lie down in like the bunk on a ship. He worked his way up onto the shelf. This left room for Slink to maneuver. The Gnome cleared cans from a shelf on his side as well. Soon he was lying down on a bunk of his own.

With Edward and Slink up on shelves, Adele had room to turn around. Her cameras had been knocked loose in the crash, and they hung down on their wires like a librarian's reading glasses. She retrieved them with her grippers, reinstalled them in their mounts, and looked the situation over. From somewhere she produced a pair of pruning snips and cut a slit high up on the deflated pool that covered the opening to the pantry. The slit was above the dead Jamook on the outside and gave them a partial view of the sky. They could see a second wave of flying Jamooks coming over the ramparts. Adele quickly clamped closed the slit in the pool and then, separating the clamp from the end of her extension arm, retreated as far as she could toward the back of the pantry.

"I guess we'll just have to wait this one out," Slink said as he took two cans of Spaghetti from the shelf above and handed one over to Edward.

For several hours they ate canned goods and listened to the sounds of destruction. Things crashed, Jamooks cursed, football bombs exploded, and buckshot rattled while the loudspeakers gave a play-by-play of the action. And then there was quiet. As it grew dark outside, the three prisoners began to look for a way out.

They reasoned, quite correctly, that there was no way they could generate enough force to move the combined dead weight of two Jamooks from the front of the pantry. Slink climbed down from his shelf and started digging into the wall of scrap that formed the rear of the pantry. "Well, one thing is for certain, we need to get some distance between us and these dead Jamooks before too much more time passes. It's been raining bloated beasts all day long, and I can tell you from experience that dead Jamooks don't keep very well at room temperature."

"I noticed they didn't smell very hygienic," Edward offered as he climbed down from his shelf as well.

"You think a live Jamook smells bad, you haven't smelled anything yet," Slink said as he pulled a small but broken flat-screen TV loose and passed it forward to Edward.

Edward took the TV and wedged it out of the way under one of the pantry shelves.

"Anyway, I was looking for the portal a few months back, working over Seasonal in Sector 2206. You remember that don't you, Adele? We were just positive that the portal, if one existed at all, was in the Seasonal Department of 2206. Anyway, I got there and was about to set up base camp when I smelled something that just about burned the hairs out of my nose."

Adele, who must have heard the story before, reached up and turned off the microphone mounted on top of her monitor.

"I just can't describe the stink. Words fail me," Slink continued undeterred. "Lucky it was near Lawn & Garden. I drug over a ten-pound sack of lime and dumped it on top of the cadaver. That made him look like a powdered doughnut but, I'm here to tell you, it did little for the stink. I had to drag over half a dozen more sacks before I made any headway with that stench. It turns out this brilliant fellow had been trying to eat the plaster fruit out of one of those wicker cow horns. You know what I'm talking about, the kind that Gnomes like to put in the middle of their Thanksgiving tables."

Slink was in the middle of passing the twisted frame from a lawn chair up to Edward when he stopped. "At least we did back when we were free people and had things to be thankful for," he said as a tear formed in his eye.

"You know what?" Edward said. "We are going to find a portal and get out of here and, when we do, you can all come over to my house for Thanksgiving dinner. It will be so much more fun with you there. And Slink, I'm sure you'll love my little brother Clemens. I don't know why I say that, but I just know it will be true. For some reason, I believe the two of you will see eye to eye."

Adele reached out two of her mechanical arms and put one around the shoulders of the boy and the other around the Gnome.

In time they came across a school backpack with a sports logo embroidered on the front, and Slink filled it with canned goods and a few utensils. The three continued to burrow through the night, taking debris from in front of them and passing it to the back. Just before dawn they broke out into the open area that had been Adele's workshop. It was hard to recognize; even Adele didn't recognize it at first. Trash was everywhere, not to mention shredded wading pools and Jamook carcasses. From one of the shelves paint, oil and cleaning fluid dripped out of cans that had been pierced by scatter-shot.

They heard a familiar buzzing sound, and a Hog appeared above the ramparts. The drone, which was listing badly, was armed with an emergency flare from Automotive. As it passed overhead the Hog lost one rotor and flipped upside down. More as a reaction than as a planned event it fired its emergency flare. The missile went almost straight up. It drifted slowly down illuminating the whole area with an eerie red light. Edward was admiring the beauty when the falling flare struck the shelf of leaking combustibles and tumbled down into the growing puddle below. The whole thing went up in a ball of flame.

CHAPTER 13

Slink and Edward hit the deck just in time as a cloud of ash and debris from the blast went over their heads. Adele was not so lucky. As one could imagine, it is difficult, if not impossible, for a robot made from a computer tower and a plastic car to duck.

When the fire had settled to a dull roar the boy and the Gnome went to inspect their robotic friend. Her cameras were, once again, displaced. Edward returned them to their mounts. He picked bits of debris off her tower and monitor, but her screen was lifeless. Slink tried the ON/OFF button, pushing it in and holding it for five seconds, but nothing happened.

"Let me see if I can find a rag to wipe some of the soot off her," Edward said as he poked around in the mess and came up with part of a beach towel.

Edward began to wipe the soot from the screen of Adele's monitor, but there was still nothing there.

"Maybe the blast knocked her connections loose," he offered.

Slink took over the rag and began to wipe down Adele's tower and pink car while Edward looked over the electrical connections in back. He removed the jumper cables from the battery, wiped the posts clean with the tail of his shirt, and replaced the cables. Slink was about to try the ON/OFF button again when they heard a loud metallic grinding sound coming from the compound wall. The two pushed their disabled friend behind a row of shelves and peered out through the clutter.

Out of the wall of rubbish on the far side of the old work room burst a full-sized lawn tractor with a Jamook at the helm. A cluster of mower blades was mounted vertically on the front of the machine, and they spun madly. Chunks of wood, plastic, and metal were flying up and over the driver's head in a rooster tail of debris. A second tractor, clearing a path for the assault, followed with a snow shovel plow attached to the prow. Behind them came a column of mounted Jamooks armed with all manner of power tools from Lawn and Garden.

Slink pushed the ON/OFF button on the robot's tower in desperation. Adele came back to life and spun her cameras completely around before directing them through an opening in the shelving the three were hiding behind. She saw the Jamook invasion and pulled back as her cameras spun again. An old black and white cartoon played across her monitor. The character in the cartoon, a cow wearing a tutu and a bell around her neck, had her mouth open so wide you could see her tonsils.

The Jamook driving the lawn tractor with the plow broke off from the column and began to circle the room clearing a pathway free of trash and dead Jamooks. Edward and Slink ducked down. The boy covered himself with a badly bent, lawn chair while Slink emptied the contents of a paper shredder over his head. Adele simply froze. The shelf they were behind held broken small appliances, crock pots, toaster ovens, vacuum cleaners and the like. By just holding still the robot managed to blend in with her surroundings. The Gnome leaned over on his side and tried his best to look discarded. The invading army passed them by.

The Jamook driving the lawn tractor with the mower blades mounted on the front circled the work area and then, picking a random spot, began to hack its way into the side wall. The Jamook with the plow lined up behind the one with the mower blades and the rank and file fell in behind them. The last one in line sprayed the remains of the fire with a shower of foam from an extinguisher. In a short while they were all gone out of sight, down through their self-made tunnel.

Adele's printer sprang to life, and a page extended out. Slink pulled the paper out and read it, "If they are coming in here then perhaps we should consider getting out."

"An excellent idea," Edward said.

The three friends waited until the convoy was little more than a distant echo and then made their move. They followed the newly made Mook trail in the opposite direction and passed through the cut the mower blades had made on the way in. The pathway was wide and clear, and they soon came out on the side of what looked to be a Jamook highway. They had no idea where they were going, but they knew that they had left Adele's compound behind for good.

With a substantial number of Jamooks dead in the aerial assault and many more engaged in the invasion, the highway, which was a good two times the size of a normal Mook Trail, was deserted.

"Which way do we go?" Slink said as he looked both up and down the highway. "I can't see where one direction is very much different than the other."

Adele spun her monitor in a circle and flashed question marks on the screen.

Edward looked both ways as well. Slink was right, there didn't seem to be much difference. "My father always said, 'When in doubt, turn left'. Although I must confess, I never understood what he was talking about."

"My mother always said, 'When in doubt, eat sauerkraut,'" Slink offered. "I'm almost certain she was talking about eating sauerkraut."

Adele spun her monitor once again and then stopped. She ran the lenses on the cameras out and the words TOURIST INFO flashed on the screen along with an arrow pointing to the right. Edward and Slink could see the blue and white sign she was pointing toward. It was too far for either of them to read, but beneath the words was a large question mark.

"I guess you'd qualify as a tourist," Slink said to Edward, "Let's go check it out."

"I'm not so sure about this," Edward said. "Tourist information centers where I come from are almost always manned by pleasant ladies who hand out brochures, maps and cups of coffee. What if this one is manned by Jamooks with no intention of welcoming us at all?"

"If Jamook tourist information centers are like everything else Jamook, I doubt there has been anybody there in years." Slink countered. "Besides, I could use a cup of coffee."

They traveled down the road in the direction the sign pointed, and after what seemed like a mile or more, the center came into view. It stood beside a small turn off and was partly buried by a cascade of debris. The center was a small alpine cottage with a steep roof line and gingerbread trim. The oversize door stood open, and several of the small, diamond-shaped panes were broken from the windows. The limited parking area was a jumble of shopping carts, all in need of repair. The little chalet was covered with moss and vines. Way above the structure, up against the roof of this strange world, a faulty sprinkler head sent a soft mist of water down over the building.

Edward heard them first, before Adele, and even before Slink.

"Drones!" he said, "I hear drones!"

CHAPTER 14

The drones came up over the distant hills behind the three compatriots. Vipers were playing their red surveillance dots over the landscape and flying in convoy with fully armed Hogs.

"Beat feet!" Slink shouted.

Slink and Edward dashed through the mist from the overhead sprinkler, skated down the slimy path and through the entrance to the Visitor's Center. They were about to slam the door behind them when they saw that Adele was still outside in the drizzle. She had lost traction; her hard, plastic wheels spinning on the slippery, green walkway. Her wheels turned slower and slower, and then stopped entirely.

The boy and the Gnome ran back out and pushed the robot into the shelter of the welcome center. The drones circled above, but no red points found the hut, and no projectiles were launched.

"Why aren't the Hogs firing? The Vipers surely have seen us," Edward said as he crawled on hands and knees over to the window and looked out. "And here comes another wave of flying Jamooks. They must have commandeered every wading pool in STUFF-4-LESS."

"It has to be the spray from the sprinklers," Slink said as he gazed up through one of the broken panes in the window. "Could be the water droplets in the air confuse their radar. As for the Jamooks, their eyesight is notoriously poor. Mostly they just follow the drones."

In a short while the drones and Jamook flotilla passed by, and Edward took the opportunity to look around the inside of the visitor's center. Although small and badly in need of attention, the interior was finely appointed with decorative molding around the windows and artistic plasterwork on the ceiling and walls. Both the counter and cupboards behind it were built with style and attention to detail. The only thing out of character was the door through which they had entered. It was so big as to appear clumsy and crudely fashioned. So badly was it fitted that the work appeared to be done with a hatchet. "With the exception of the front door this doesn't look at all like Jamook craftsmanship," he said.

"It's not. Jamooks couldn't stack pancakes two high without them falling over," Slink said as he sized up a dust covered coffee vending machine. "This Visitor's Center was built by Free Gnomes back in the days before Fearon came to power. The Jamooks cut that door because they couldn't fit through the old one." Slink selected a spot just above the coin slot and struck it sharply with his fist. A small, tin coin dropped into the return tray.

"The front door aside, it certainly looks like fine workmanship." Edward said.

Slink examined the coin and then tossed it aside. "We Free Gnomes are known as superior artisans capable of fine and delicate work," he said as he balanced briefly on his hands and mule-kicked the side of the machine with both feet. The front of the vending machine fell off onto the floor.

"What does Fearon look like?" Edward asked as he found a red, souvenir T-shirt behind the counter and began to wipe the water from Adele.

"The most horrid creature of all," Slink said as he searched the inside of the vending machine. "Fearon the Feared, better you never meet him."

Edward wiped the last of the water from the robot and tossed the shirt onto an overstuffed chair that was torn and losing its stuffing. "I think Adele has turned herself off," he said.

"Try that on-off thing," the Slink offered.

Edward tried the button to no avail. He dried the connections to the battery but that was of no help either. "I'm quite sure her battery has run down," he said.

"She has a little box she plugs in and recharges herself, but I think it's in her workshop, or what used to be her workshop," Slink said as he sifted through the litter in the bottom of the vending machine and found an envelope of instant coffee. "But she might carry it with her. I'm not sure."

Edward looked around Adele's pink car and found a small door on one of the back fenders. Inside was a battery charger. He pushed the robot behind the counter, plugged the charger into an outlet in the back wall, unhooked her jumper cables and hooked up the charger. A red light on the charger began to blink. "This could take quite a while," he said.

Slink opened the packet of coffee, wet his finger, and stuck it first in the coffee and then in his mouth. "Anything of value behind the counter there?" he asked.

Edward found a small wicker basket half filled with packets of sugar and non-dairy creamer. He slid the basket across the counter to Slink. "Some T-shirts, bubble wrap, and half-a-dozen foam rubber beer can coolers. There are a bunch of brochures back here as well. 'Welcome to STUFF-4-LESS. stuff You Don't Need at Prices You Can Afford.'" he read from the front of one of the pamphlets.

Slink opened several packets of both creamer and sugar and dumped them into the coffee envelope. He shook up the bag and poured a generous helping into his mouth. "Is there a map in that brochure?" he asked through a spray of powder.

Edward handed several of the pamphlets across the counter to Slink, and he took one and looked it over.

"This is a Jamook publication. The design is primitive, the layout is awkward, and the color registration is way off," he said. "But there's a map on the back page."

Edward came out from behind the counter, and the two studied the map. "Do you know where we are?" he asked.

Slink pointed to a red star on the map. "It says we are here, but I'm not familiar with this part of the country, and that ignorance is by choice. We're in the belly of the beast, and I've always made a habit of giving this territory a wide berth. Fearon's headquarters can't be too far from here," he said. "I wonder what these numbers on the map stand for?"

Edward picked up one of the brochures as well. "There's a numbered list of tourist attractions inside. I bet they correspond to the numbers on the map," he said.

"We aren't far from number three," Slink pointed out. "What do they say is there?"

"Let's see," the boy said as he flipped the pamphlet open. "Number one is the Jamook water park, but I think we can skip that. Those beasts smell bad enough when they are dry. Here it is, number three, Flamingo Petting Zoo."

"That must be where they're holding the flamingos," Slink said as he poured some more of the coffee mixture into his mouth. "What's at number six and number seven? They're somewhat past number three and just across from each other on the Mook Trail."

"Number six is the Jamook incubator, and seven is, let's see, number seven seems to be a wildlife enclosure of some sort called Gnome on the Range."

Slink expelled a shower of coffee, sugar and creamer. "Gnome on the Range. That's got to be the Free Gnome concentration camp."

As he spoke the room was filled with a flash of green light, and one of the remaining windows of the cottage shattered in a spray of glass.

CHAPTER 15

There was another flash of light. Another pane of glass shattered sending a shower of shards across the room. By this time Edward was behind the counter and trying to fumble his pricer out of his pocket. He dropped the weapon, and it bounced out toward the middle of the room.

Jamooks could be heard talking in their gruff, unintelligible tongue and laughing. Edward had never heard a Jamook laugh before and thought it sounded halfway between a seal bark and a root beer burp. The kind of burp you would expect if you were to drink an entire can of root beer all at once - warm root beer.

Slink, who was hiding behind the vending machine, dropped to the floor and began to crawl over to Edward's position. "Be careful of the glass," the boy cautioned.

Slink picked up the pricer as he came. He reached the counter and returned the weapon to the boy. Slink then picked up a large splinter of glass, stuck it into his mouth and began to crunch. "Gnome glass. It's made from spun sugar," he explained.

"How long before they attack?" Edward said as he waved the pricer around.

"I don't think you'll be needing that," Slink said as he pushed the weapon to the side. "I speak a little Jamookese, and I think they were just pausing to take pot shots at the windows as they rode by."

There were no more shots fired, and soon Edward could hear the Mookmobiles fade into the distance. From the far-off sounds of football bombs exploding, he could tell the invasion of Adele's compound was still going on. The boy rose to his feet and began to practice his quick-draw.

"Pricers only fire a few times before they need to be recharged," Slink pointed out. "Don't waste it."

"The light on Adele's charger is still blinking red," Edward said as he returned the weapon to his pocket and tentatively picked up a glass shard from the top of the counter. He touched it to his tongue and was pleasantly surprised.

"It'll be dark in an hour or two, and then we'll have the advantage. It looks like Jamooks have headlights on their new tractors, but their vision isn't good even in daylight; at night they are pretty near blind," Slink said. "Still, if we're going to travel Mook trails then we'll need some sort of disguises. Let's see what we can find while we still have some light."

Edward began to sort through the items behind the counter. "Like I said, there are some STUFF-4-LESS shirts back here," he said as he held up an expansive yellow one. "All extra-large and bigger."

Slink was rummaging through the closet at the back of the cottage. He stuck his head out to look at the shirt. "Any other colors?" he asked.

"Let's see," the boy said as he thumbed through the shirts. "One red, two yellow, four blue and two green,"

"Two green? Just what shade of green would you say they were?" Slink replied as he ducked back into the closet.

"Well, not lime Jell-O, that's for sure," Edward said as he held up one of the dirty green shirts. "These are long-sleeve T-shirts."

"Apple green?" Slink offered.

"Not apple, and not lettuce or celery, not anything a person would care to eat. I'd say they were more like asparagus or maybe even lizard."

"Lizard green sounds perfect," Slink said as he reappeared with a string mop in his hand. He draped the mop head over the top of Adele's monitor. "I think she'll make a very pretty Jamookette."

Edward and Slink got the bubble wrap from behind the counter and wrapped several layers around Adele's tower while being careful to leave access to her power button. They found a pair of scissors in a drawer and cut slits from the neck down to the shoulders of one of the green shirts so they could pull it over her monitor. Once the shirt was in place they fastened the slits back together with a stapler that they found in the same drawer as the scissors. Edward rolled up some of the bubble wrap and stuffed the sleeves of the T-shirt. Slink removed the mop head from its handle and draped it over the robot's monitor being careful not to disturb the artificial sunflower on top of her microphone.

Edward found a dustpan and a broom in the closet. He pushed the broom handle down one of Adele's sleeves and into the pink car that served as her base and means of locomotion. The robot seemed to be executing a permanent stiff-armed salute. Slink fastened the dustpan to the other arm. The two cleaning implements replicated a Jamook's large hands and webbed fingers.

"Not too shabby, if I do say so myself," Slink said as they stepped back to admire the finished product.

Edward was somewhat more skeptical. "Just how bad is a Jamook's eyesight?"

"Like I said, at night they are practically blind," Slink said as he adjusted the bubble wrap inside one of Adele's false arms.

"In that case, I think it would be for the best if we try to travel at night as much as we can," the boy said.

"One down, two to go," Slink said.

There was a back door to the visitor's center that had never been enlarged to accommodate Jamooks. The friends eased it open and looked out. The mountain of trash behind the building nearly covered what had once been an attractive garden of flowerbeds and greenery. Fed by the constant misting from the sprinkler head, the plants had grown wild and tangled among the rubbish.

There was a small storage shed attached to the back of the cottage. The shed, pressed hard by the avalanche of debris, listed badly to one side. The door was jammed, and it was only with some effort that Slink and Edward managed to force it open. Inside were rusted gardening tools, paint supplies, boxes of

Christmas decorations, and a badly damaged artificial tree.

"Perhaps we can go with a Christmas theme," Edward suggested as he worked the tree loose and drug it out into what was left of the yard. "We're lucky it's almost Thanksgiving and well into the Christmas season."

"What's the Christmas season?" Slink said as he slid the decoration boxes out into the yard as well.

"It's the run-up to Christmas," the boy explained as he took a plastic bag of broken ornaments from one of the boxes and tossed it aside. "It once started right after Thanksgiving, but it keeps getting earlier every year. Now the Christmas decorations go in the stores at the same time as the Halloween candy."

"Since Fearon took over, we don't have a Christmas season anymore, or any other kind of a season for that matter," Slink said as he took a small artificial wreath from another box and held it up so he could view Edward through the hole in the center.

"All our holidays go on simultaneously. It's just one big party here in STUFF-4-LESS; 24-7-365. The pressure to buy is relentless."

"Let's get these things inside, out of the drizzle, and see what we can do with it," Edward said.

Once they were inside with their swag, Slink fitted the wreath on top of Edward's head and then found a shiny plastic star and mounted it on the front. "I think you will make a very handsome Christmas tree," he said.

Edward removed the longer branches from the artificial tree and fastened them up under his belt, forming what looked like an evergreen hula skirt. Slink wove the shorter branches into a mantle, which he fitted around the boy's shoulders. Edward lifted the vending machine door up and looked at his reflection in the glass. "I guess I look more like a Christmas tree than I do like a fire hydrant," he conceded.

"Well, that's two down," Slink said as he made some last-minute adjustments to Edward's greenery.

"But I don't know any easy way to disguise a Gnome. We are such distinguished characters."

Edward found a red Christmas stocking in one of the boxes. It was a large sock with white furry trim around the top edge. The boy removed the Gnome's pointed hat and stretched the stocking down over it. "I think you'll make a lovely Santa," he said as he replaced the hat on Slink's head.

Slink looked at his reflection in the glass, snatched the hat off his head, and threw it to the ground. "This is an embarrassment," he said. "Gnomes don't look anything like Santa Clause."

The boy picked up the stocking, brushed off the sugar glass shards, and handed it back to Slink. "Gnomes look very much like Santa, and we do have to try and free the Flamingos and the other Free Gnomes. Why don't you go into the closet and look through the cleaning supplies? Perhaps you can find something in there that will whiten a beard. I'll try to come up with the rest of your outfit."

Slink reluctantly put the stocking covered hat back on his head and went into the storeroom. In short order, came out with a gallon of bleach and a scrub brush. He went into the bathroom and closed the door behind himself.

Edward went back behind the counter and sorted once more through the shelves and drawers. The one red shirt back there was way too big for their purposes, but then he remembered the smaller one he had dried Adele off with. He found it where he had tossed it on the chair with the torn fabric. The label said it was a medium, and Edward laid it out on the countertop. It was streaked with soot and still damp in spots. STUFF-4-LESS was screen printed in silver ink across the front. "Well, my father always says, it's an imperfect world," he mused.

Edward found some craft paste in one of the drawers and pulled a double handful of dirty white stuffing from the split chair. He spread the paste around the hem of the T-shirt and stuck the chair stuffing in the paste. He smeared a wide band up the front of the shirt and stuck stuffing there as well. It did an adequate job of distracting from the silver screen printing. He cut the bottoms off the foam beer can coolers and attached them like oversized buttons.

Slink came out of the bathroom just as Edward was finishing up. His beard, which had been chestnut brown, was now off white and streaked with dingy yellow. He smelled heavily of bleach. Together they worked Slink into the red shirt and placed the stocking back on his head. It came down almost to his shoe tops. Edward ran a belt of silver duct tape around the waist. "I think you look just fine," the boy said.

The light on Adele's charger had changed from blinking red to steady green. "I think she's fully charged," Edward said. The boy disconnected the charger and replaced it in its compartment. He reconnected the jumper cables and pushed the ON/OFF button. Adele sprang back to life. She spun her monitor around and pivoted her cameras taking in both the boy and the Gnome. A huge smile took up most of her screen interspersed with scenes of people laughing. "We're in disguise," Edward explained.

Adele turned her cameras once again and caught sight of her own reflection in the vending machine glass. A cartoon of a steam whistle with bulging eyes filled her display. "You're in disguise as well," Slink pointed out. The steam whistle spun as it intensified its output, its eyes bulging even further until its top blew. Finally, it was spent and sagged with its tongue out.

"I think she took that well," Slink said.

Edward found a small decorative waste basket with daisies painted on the sides. He eased it over Adele's artificial flower and microphone and settled it down in place. Adele looked once again at her image in the glass. The smile returned to her monitor, and she adjusted the inverted waste basket to a rakish angle.

"Can you get a picture of a Jamook on your screen?" Edward asked Adele.

Adele flashed through a series of photos of Jamooks who had fallen off their carts and were lying in embarrassing positions or ones that were obviously dead.

"I was thinking of a full screen, head shot," Edward explained.

Adele complied. A photo of an ugly, green Jamook filled her display. The effect was somewhat believable if one squinted real hard.

It was now dark, as dark as things ever get in STUFF-4-LESS. A shadowy darkness infused with the glow from countless red EXIT signs and low wattage emergency lights. "Listen here, Edward," Slink said to the boy. "I have to do all I can to rescue the other Free Gnomes, and Adele will go with me I'm for certain, but you don't have to. Between the Jamooks and Fearon it could be very dangerous. In fact, I'm sure it will be."

"I have never seen a real live pink flamingo, or Gnomes in their natural habitat, for that matter," Edward said as he drew his pricer and spun it clumsily around on his finger. "There is no way I'm going to pass up this opportunity."

The three ventured out and started down the Mook Trail in the direction of the Flamingo Petting Zoo and Gnome on the Range. They had gone only a few hundred feet when a bright light froze them in their tracks.

CHAPTER 16

Frozen they were and frozen they stayed. "Let Adele handle this," Slink said under his breath. As Edward's eyes adjusted, he could make out two Jamooks squatting behind a spotlight. They spoke in their loud and gruff language. Out of the corner of his eye he could see Adele's monitor. The big smile icon was superimposed over the photo of the Jamook. The two sentries laughed their barking laugh and growled some more. A blush red came over the face on the robot's screen. The Jamooks smirked and poked each other in the ribs. The photo on Adele's display switched rapidly to a Jamook with one eye closed and back again. The Jamooks roared, their laughter even louder this time, as they moved out of the trail and returned Adele's stiff-armed salute. The three travelers hurried on.

"What happened back there," Edward asked as soon as they were out of ear shot of the Jamook check point.

"Adele doesn't speak, but she's programmed herself to understand several languages," Slink explained. "One of them is Jamookese. I didn't understand every word, but I believe they thought she was Christmas shopping. They paid her some rude compliments, and she batted her eyes at them. Long story short, we were waved through."

"What's our next move?" Edward asked as he took the brochure from his jacket pocket and looked at the map by the light of Adele's monitor.

"Let's take a look at Gnome on the Range. If we can free some of the Gnomes, we can gain allies and cause confusion at the same time," Slink said.

They started back down the Mook Trail and soon came to the Flamingo Petting Zoo. The zoo was surrounded with wire fencing and covered over with a low canopy of patchwork netting. In places the netting hung down low and was propped up by tent poles and mop handles. All was quiet. Dozens of birds stood on one leg around the edges of an artificial pond filled with dirty water.

"They stand on one leg when they sleep," Slink explained.

Further on they came to the Jamook Incubator. Through the metal bars of the fence Edward could see that dozens of large fish tanks were precariously stacked five or six high along every wall. Water from a haphazard series of garden hoses, that were attached to the sprinkler system above, fed a trickle of water down into the top tanks. From there the water overflowed and fed the next tank down. The water running over from tank number two filled tank number three and so forth until it reached the bottom. The tanks got larger, and the water darker as things progressed from top to bottom.

The water in the top tanks was somewhat clear and Edward could see tadpole-like creatures about the size of frisbees. They had long tails, fins and the facial feature of Jamooks; cute little Jamooks. The second tank down in each stack had somewhat larger tadpoles with more developed appendages and more repulsive features. The water was also dirtier. The pattern was repeated all the way down to the bottom tanks, which were quite large and held water that was thick and greenish brown in color. Large, dark, shadowy forms could be seen moving behind the slime covered glass. Each tank was wired with a monitor that hung on the edge and extended down into the water.

"That's the Mook Mincer," Slink said as he pointed to one end of the enclosure where there was a large machine with a hopper on top and a forklift parked beside it. "The Mincer grinds up dead Jamooks and spits out Mook Kibble that's fed to the ..."

"Look, there's Gnome on the Range," Edward said, eager to change the subject.

Across the Mook Trail from the Incubator was another area that was surrounded by a tall, chain-link fence topped by coils of barbed wire. The only way into the fenced area appeared to be a reinforced steel gate with an electronic lock. Just outside of the fence there was a ramp that led up to an observation platform. The three compatriots ascended the ramp.

Gnome on the Range stood in stark contrast to the Jamook Incubator and, for that matter, the rest of STUFF-4-LESS. It was clean and well organized. Orderly streets passed between tidy rows of shelves that were sparsely but neatly stocked. Interspersed among the shelves were open, park-like spaces with play structures. Many of the streets were lined with steep roofed cottages that were built in the same architectural style as the tourist welcome center. These little houses were all immaculately maintained with raised beds of flowers growing in front and vegetable gardens in the rear. Cameras mounted on top of the surrounding fence monitored the scene.

"Can those cameras see us?" Edward asked.

"I don't believe they can. I think they are all trained down into the compound," Slink replied. "But to be on the safe side, we best not stay up here too long."

They were halfway down the ramp when Slink heard someone whisper his name. He turned and looked at Edward; Edward looked right back at him. They both shrugged their shoulders. "Slink," the voice came again, this time a little louder. It was clearly coming from beneath the observation platform. They descended the rest of the ramp and turned into the darkness beneath the platform. There, on the other side of the chain-link fence, they could see the outline of a Gnome.

"The years have not been good to you my brother," the shadowy Gnome said.

"Clink, could that be you?" Slink said as he stroked his yellow-white beard.

"We knew you would come for us if you could," the Gnome in the shadows said and then took a step backward and into the light. She was perhaps an inch shorter and had no beard but, other than that, looked remarkably like Slink.

"This is my sister, Cassandra Lorraine Irene Natalia Kinkaid," Slink said by way of introduction. "And this is Edward. He came through the portal from BUY-N-BULK."

"So, you found it, my brother," Clink replied. "We had all but given up hope that such a thing existed."

"Clink," Edward exclaimed. "I saw the painting you did of your brother in Topside. It was really quite remarkable considering what you had to work with."

Slink folded his arms across his chest and looked down his nose at Edward.

"I'm talking about materials, Ketchup and mustard and such, not subject matter," Edward clarified.

"Thank you," Cassandra said as she stepped close to the fence again and back into the shadows. "This is a blind spot; the cameras can't see us here. We post a sentry at this point every night to watch and listen. The Incubator is a very popular meeting place for young Jamooks. The males like to brag about their exploits and the females like to gossip."

"Do tell me, my sister, what have you seen and what have you heard?" Slink asked as he stepped forward toward Clink.

"Be careful of the fence; it carries an electrical charge," Clink said. "I'm sure you've noticed there is an all-out attack going on. You can hear it if you listen for the sounds. They do this every few years. Jamook attackers are like neighborhood dogs barking; one starts, and they all start even though none of them knows what they are barking at. It just goes on until they are all barked out.

"I know what they are barking at, I mean, attacking," Edward said with some pride. "They are attacking us."

"You three are doing very well, my young friend," Clink said. "By all reports the Jamooks are taking heavy casualties, mostly self-inflicted, I am sure, since you are all here. The Free Gnomes are ready to join the fight and inflict some casualties of our own, but this perimeter fence is impenetrable."

"What can we do to help?" Edward asked.

"Someone must get into Fearon's Command Center and disable the lights, cameras, and electric fence," Clink said. "We have bolt cutters and an arsenal of homemade weapons. Shutdown security here at Gnome on the Range, and we can take it from there."

"We will do it," both Edward and Slink said at the same time.

Clink rolled up a sheet of paper and, being careful not to touch the metal links, extended it through the fence. Slink took it.

"On that paper is a map that will take you to Fearon's Command Center. It's not far from here," she said. "On the bottom of the paper is the entry code, password, cipher, encrypted secret key, and access symbols you will need to get into the computer."

Slink handed the paper to Edward. "This sounds like your department," he said.

"How did you get this information?" Edward asked as he studied the paper.

"We watch, we listen, and it doesn't hurt that Fearon has no choice but to use Gnomes for his tech support," Clink said. "Once you get into the computer you will need to disable the fence security and the electronic lock on the gate."

"Is Fearon's computer an Apple or a PC?" Edward asked. "I've worked with both but I'm more comfortable with Apple."

"I don't know either of those names; they must be BUY-N-BULK computers," Clink confessed. "Coincidentally, we also have two types here in STUFF-4-LESS, Data Grinders and Smelts. DGs are more versatile, but Smelts are more popular. I must admit I have little experience with either."

Adele entered the conversation for the first time by printing out a page. Slink took the paper and read from it. "She says that she can access the user's guide for both Smelt and Data Grinder."

"That will be all you should need," Clink said as she looked at Adele and smiled. "By the way, I don't believe you are either a Data Grinder or a Smelt."

Adele flashed her biggest smile.

"She built herself with components from the Electronics Department," Edward said, showing great pride in his friend.

"Well, you did a wonderful job, and I think your flowered hat is beautiful," Clink said.

"I don't mean to interrupt," Slink said. "But what will Fearon be doing while we stroll into his Command Center and start fooling around with his computer?"

"We will need a distraction," Edward offered up. As he spoke, he became aware of a sound coming from the direction of the battlefield. "It's a drone and it sounds like it's damaged."

The boy was right. A Viper with a bad engine limped into view over the Jamook Incubator. As they watched, the engine cut out completely and the drone fell into one of the tanks. There was a splash of brackish water; lights came on all around the tank walls, and a siren sounded a whooping yowl.

CHAPTER 17

"Get as far back under the ramp as you can," Clink said as she ducked down farther into the shadows.

The three warriors complied, and in a matter of minutes a column of half-a-dozen Jamooks came roaring up from the direction of Fearon's headquarters. The first one in line swiped a pass card through the electronic lock on the gate, and they all filed into the Incubator enclosure.

The creatures circled their carts around and around, banging into tanks and splashing water out onto the already wet floor. Young Jamooks of every size roiled in their containers. Some of the smaller hatchlings flipped out of their own tanks and into the tanks below where they were quickly devoured. Others splashed out onto the floor and were run over by Mookmobiles.

Finally, one of the emergency responders located the drone that set off the alarm and ladled it out of the tank with one of its big flat hands. The creatures laughed it up and played catch with the defunct Viper. When they tired of the game, the leader of the pack slapped his hand on a big red button against the wall, and the sirens and flashing lights stopped. The Jamooks filed back out of the Incubator and pulled the gate shut behind them.

When the Jamook platoon was gone, Slink, Edward and Adele came out of hiding and resumed their conference with Clink.

"Does this happen often?" Slink asked.

"They have an 'event' of some kind at the incubator once a week or so," Clink said. "Mostly they are false alarms. The big red button turns off the alarms and signals 'all clear' to the Command Center. Once it jammed, and dozens of Jamooks showed up along with Fearon himself."

"So, if we could set off the alarm and jam the red button it would create enough of a distraction to bring Fearon out of his command post?" Edward said.

"That it might, but how do we set off the alarm and then jam the button?" Clink asked.

"Could you do it with a pricer?" Edward said as he whipped the weapon out of his pocket and twirled it expertly around his finger.

"Yes," Clink said as she eyed the electronic shooter. "Go back up to the observation platform and see if you can throw it over the top of the wire."

Edward went back up the ramp, and when he reached the top, readied for the throw. "Here it comes," he said in as loud a whisper as he could manage. He tossed the weapon up. It hung momentarily in the coil of barbed wire at the top and then fell. Clink caught it just before it hit the ground.

"OK, got it," she said.

"It may only have two or three shots left, four at the most," Slink said as he eyed the target across the street. "This won't be an easy shot to start with. The effective range of a pricer is about 50 feet, and the laser beam may bounce off the glass of the tank if you don't hit it straight on. Take out one of the tanks first, one of the big ones. That will set off the alarm. Once the alarm sounds, aim for the red button."

"Understood," Clink said.

"What time does Fearon get to the Command Center in the morning?" Edward asked as he returned to the group.

"Precisely at 7:00 AM," Clink said. "We're in luck. The Jamooks usually come for us at 7:00 as well, but because of the current military action they have us in lock-down."

"7:00 AM sounds good to me. No use wasting time," Slink said.

"Let's give him time to power up his computer," Edward said as he looked at the extensive list of passwords and access codes. "Maybe we can get him to do some of this work for us."

"How about 7:15," Clink said as she checked her watch. "You have about three hours before dawn.

That should be plenty of time to get close to Fearon's Command Center and find a hiding place."

"How will we know what it looks like?" Edward asked.

"You will know it. It's a glass box in the sky above the plaza with the ugly statue in the center of it," Clink said

"But what do we do if Fearon locks the door when he leaves?" Edward asked.

Slink and Clink looked at each other and back at Edward. "It has no lock," Clink explained. "No one would ever be foolish enough to enter Fearon's Command Center."

"And, my brother," Clink added as she ducked back into the shadows. "That Santa look is not a good one for you."

Within half-an-hour the Mook Highway opened into a large but junk-strewn plaza. Flag poles, some bent and some absent of flags, ringed the area. The flags that were present were all tattered and featured the STUFF-4-LESS motto. On one side of the plaza there was a park with a dented metal picnic table missing one of its benches and a few aluminum lawn chairs with the fiberglass webbing in shreds. A basketball backboard without a hoop, a swing set with no swings and a most unsanitary looking sand box comprised an unfortunate playground.

In the center of the plaza was a leaky fountain that caused a swath of greenish slime to spread across one side of the square. In the center of the fountain was a statue of a small man in glasses. It was crudely carved from inferior stone and covered with bird droppings.

High above the far end of the plaza was a structure about the size of a boxcar. It was fitted on all sides with large windows that afforded a panoramic view of STUFF-4-LESS. The booth stood on stilts with its only access by means of a long metal staircase that doubled back on itself like the steps up to a fire tower.

"We better find a hole to hide in and get some rest," Slink said as he surveyed the plaza.

They were in luck for just beneath the steps to the glass booth was a pile of discarded Christmas decorations, wreaths, yard ornaments, and artificial trees. It was a bit of luck but not a total surprise. Piles of discarded Christmas decorations were not a rarity in STUFF-4-LESS. Slink and Edward nestled into the mound of holiday discards and were quickly asleep.

Adele, who could make herself practically invisible anywhere in the store where broken household items were found, and that was almost everywhere, backed into an opening in some nearby junk and shifted herself into power-saver mode.

Edward was dreaming of his home when he was awakened by Adele powering up. He could also hear the sound of an approaching vehicle. It was not the loud, badly tuned sound of a Mookmobile but the smooth hum of an electric motor. Edward peeked out through the artificial foliage just as a golf cart braked sharply to a stop right in front of his hiding place. The cart rocked as a life form stepped out.

"That, my friend, is Fearon," Slink whispered in reverent tones.

Edward looked up in disbelief.

CHAPTER 18

What Edward was looking at was not the monster of epic proportions that he was led to believe. In fact, it was not a monster at all but a man, a little man at that. From what the boy could see from his place of concealment, the small man looked to be wearing a dark suit, white shirt and a conservative necktie. His shoes, which were most plainly visible, were wingtips and his socks argyle. In his white gloved hands was a pocket calculator. Edward was sure it was the man portrayed by the unfortunate statue in the center of the plaza fountain.

"That's Fearon the Feared?" the boy whispered as the small man passed just feet from their position and started up the steps. "That's the creature everybody in STUFF-4-LESS is frightened of?" As he spoke, he could hear Fearon stumble on the stairs and then catch his balance.

Edward started up out of the cover of the greenery, but Slink pulled him back down. "Fearon has great powers," he said as they listened to the man make his way up the flights of metal steps and open the door to the Command Center at the top.

"How did someone like that end up running the show?" Edward asked when he felt it was safe to talk. "In my land we call people like him 'bean counters. And he's a man. Not a Gnome.'"

"I don't know how it happened to happen or how he got here. But you're right, he's a person like you, only somewhat bigger. I can see that now. I'm not sure anybody can say for certain how he got here. Maybe he was trying to get a jug of milk from the back of the cooler."

"So, he came through the portal from BUY-N-BULK?"

Slink seemed not to hear as he stared off into the distance. "I've heard it said that children remember things from their childhood being much bigger than they really were. For me, the world was a much smaller place; or, at least, it seemed to be. This territory wasn't called STUFF-4-LESS back then; we just referred to it as our Gnomeland. In Gnomeland there was room for all, and meaningful work to be had.

"My father worked at the railroad station, Gnome Depot. I always went by there after school because he would give me a nickel to get a cookie at Gnome Sweet Gnome, the bakery next to the station." Slink's narrative trailed off.

"And then Fearon came?" Edward offered to keep the story going.

"Yes, Fearon came," Slink said as he looked up at the bottom of the Command Center. "He was just meant to be an efficiency expert. He was supposed to help us."

"But somehow he took power?" The boy asked.

"He didn't take power, we gave it to him," Slink said as he settled back. "Fearon started making suggestions. Mind you, these were just suggestions about how we could improve productivity and profit, stuff like that. Some Gnomes took his advice, and it seemed to work for them. Before long he was advising all the most successful Gnomes. There was, for the first time, competition where once there was cooperation.

"In time Fearon took over the bookkeeping for a few of the Gnomes. We are a race of artists, and almost to the man, hate working with numbers. Those individuals who turned their finances over to Fearon started doing better than those who did their own books. Soon he was doing the books for half of Gnomeland, and that half profited. The land became divided.

"His powers grew slowly, and before any of us knew what was happening, we were powerless against him. Not even the Department of Gnomeland Security could help," Slink said as he looked down. "We have no one to blame but ourselves. We got lazy.

Fearon was willing to take over our lives, and we were perfectly willing to let him. Our quality of life went down as our gross national product went up."

"I'd say that 'gross' would be the key word," Edward said as he looked out over the plaza. "Once you saw what was happening did you try to fight back?"

"Yes, we organized peaceful protests," Slink said. "But Fearon convinced the more affluent Gnomes that the protesters were a danger to them and their new-found status. He had them take down the names of all who joined the movement, and before the demonstrators knew what was happening their jobs were eliminated. They had to find another position. Down-sizing it was called. Gnomes who were fine craftsmen, some of the best in the land, were reduced to stocking shelves. The leaders were put in the camp you saw, Gnome on the Range"

Edward, seeing his friend so saddened, was working up quite a temper. "My father calls himself a product of the 1960s. 'Sometimes', he says, 'peaceful protest just isn't enough'. He usually follows that with a speech about gears and levers and an odious machine, but I must confess, I never understood that part. Particularly the word odious."

"Sounds like something that smells bad," Slink said as he hung his head and shook it slowly back and forth. "Soon any Gnome who questioned Fearon or his policies was put in the camp. We launched an armed rebellion, but it was too late. Fearon had retooled the motorized shopping carts and transformed the comical Jamooks into a brutal fighting force. He turned them lose on us and we were hopelessly overmatched."

Adele interrupted the conversation by opening yet another door in her pink car and taking out a Weasel which she handed to Slink. The Gnome crawled out and under the golf cart where he fastened the small painted box to the underside of the machine.

At precisely 7:15 the sound of sirens could be heard coming from the distant direction of the Jamook Incubator. "Right on time," Slink said.

Fearon could be heard scurrying around in the observation room above. "What's our plan?" Edward asked.

"When he leaves, you go up to the Command Center and find out what's the story with the computer. I'll stay down here with Adele. It would be great to have her up there as well, but we would be half a day getting her up those stairs," Slink said. "She will have to stay down here with me. She can print out instructions and I can holler them up to you."

Above them the scurrying became more frantic, and then Fearon burst out onto the metal staircase. His polished wingtips made much more noise coming back down than they did on the way up. Slink and Edward ducked back even farther into the pile of Christmas debris, and Adele turned off her monitor and powered down.

Fearon hit the bottom of the stairs and was just about to climb into his golf cart when he stopped and looked slowly around. His gaze passed over the hiding place for the boy and the Gnome and then scanned past the robot as well. Edward breathed a sigh of relief as Fearon was once again on the verge of leaving.

But then he stopped again and riveted his focus on Adele who had shifted back to energy-saver mode. Fearon reached in and got a pricer from off the dashboard of his cart. He adjusted some dials on the top of it, aimed it at Adele, and pulled the trigger.

CHAPTER 19

Edward started to jump out of the green cover beneath the steps, but Slink, once again, pulled him down. "Hold on," the Gnome cautioned.

Rather than shooting out a laser beam of green light, the weapon in Fearon's hand just whirred and spit out a strip of paper. It was a bar-code sticker which the small man peeled off its backing and attached firmly to Adele's screen. Having completed the task, the bean counter climbed into his golf cart and sped away.

"Fearon's pricer can set prices," Slink said when the cart was out of sight. "In his hands a bar code printer can be more dangerous than a gun."

"We better get this sticker off Adele before she sees it," Edward said. He peeled off the bar-code just as she was coming back up to full power.

"Fearon's gone, but he may not be gone for long. We need to move quickly," Slink said.

Edward scurried up the metal steps and found the door unlocked. Once inside he looked around for the computer. The room was full of vintage furniture. A roll top desk, two overstuffed chairs, a large wardrobe with mirrored doors, a heavy wooden side table with a vase of fresh flowers, and a piano all competed for attention. He opened the top of the desk but found only papers, envelopes, pamphlets and dozens of books, mostly on accounting and business theory.

The upper part of the wardrobe was empty, but in the drawers were dozens of pairs of argyle socks and white gloves along with a pricer. He couldn't tell if it was the kind that shot lasers or the kind that printed bar codes. Edward checked its gauge and saw that it had only one charge left. He twirled it around his finger and put it in his jacket pocket.

The piano caught his attention. It was larger than normal and seemed to be made from cast iron. There was a stove pipe coming from the top and going out through the ceiling of the room. He had to use both hands but managed to lift the cover off the keys. The metal felt oddly warm. Numbers, letters, and symbols were handwritten with permanent markers on every key.

He opened the iron doors above the keyboard and found a monitor the size of a goldfish bowl. Next to the keyboard was a chromium microphone which looked like a thermos bottle welded to an electric stove burner. Edward pressed one of the keys on the piano, and a note sounded. The monitor came to life, and the outline of a fish bounced across the screen.

The boy stepped back out onto the landing and signaled down to Adele and Slink. "The computer is still on, and I believe it's a Smelt, but it doesn't have a mouse."

"Good, good, we don't want any mice," Slink said as he took a page from Adele's printer and read it up to Edward. "Press the key with the red STOP sign, and when the menu comes up, use the arrow keys to navigate. Go to START, and then scroll down to

BEGIN. From there go down to COMMENCE, and then down to LAUNCH, and from there down to INITIATE."

"I think this is going to be very much like our computers back home," Edward said as he ducked back into the control room and set about following Slink's instructions. He began to key in the directions he had been given, and as he did, musical notes sounded with each stroke. When he reached INITIATE, he went back to the door at the top of the steps and got his next set of instructions.

"Go to MENU and down to CHOICES," Slink read from the next sheet. "From CHOICES, down to SELECTIONS, and then to OPTIONS....

The sirens from the direction of the Jamook Incubator stopped. The silence was profound.

".... and then to SECURITY," the Gnome concluded.

Edward dashed back into the command room with a new sense of urgency. He began to run through his latest set of instructions, but the light of the primitive computer's screen began to dim. He checked for a loose connection but could not find a power cord at all.

He ran back to the door. "The thing is shutting down," he said in a near panic.

Adele whirred and burbled, and a sheet of paper came out of her printer slot. Slink hastily retrieved it. "She needs the model number. According to this diagram it's down low on the back," Slink said as he held up the paper.

The boy dashed back in, got down on his hands and knees, and twisted his head, as best he could, to see into the narrow space behind the computer. There were numbers there alright, embossed in the iron plating. They were about halfway down the length of the machine and could not be read from Edward's angle. He lay down flat on the floor and reached as far back as his arm would allow. From this position he could trace the numbers with his finger. The metal was very warm, bordering on hot, but he could read the numbers like they were written in Braille.

Back outside he called the numbers down to Adele, "S,1,0,1,"

The robot was quick with her response and Slink reported the results. "It's an older model Smelt. The first ones were coal fired."

"Cold fired? How can fire be cold?"

"Not cold, coal, C O A L,"

"Like the stuff bad kids get in their stockings?"

"It's also a rock that can burn," Slink said as he looked back down at the latest diagram that was printed on the sheet. "Under the keyboard is a door and inside that door is the firebox. You need to stoke the fire back up. Use coal if you can find it. If not, anything that will burn will have to do."

Edward rushed back inside and looked around for coal, although he wasn't even sure he would recognize it. He found none.

He got down and pulled the fire door open. The coals were still glowing but just barely. He went over to the roll top desk and took out as many of the business management books as he could carry. One fell to the floor, and he was just about to kick it toward the piano when he stopped short. It was a pink grade school folder with kittens on the cover. He kicked it out of his way, and it fell open to the page where Adele had marked the location of the portal with the big red X.

Edward couldn't stop. He hauled the other books over to the computer and fed them, one by one, into the fire. He stacked in as many volumes as would fit and then blew on the coals until the books burst into flame. The computer came back to life.

"SELECTIONS to OPTIONS to SECURITY," he said to himself, and he ran his fingers over the keys. There was something familiar in the arrangement of notes the piano played as he punched in the instructions. It was almost a tune, a tune he recognized.

He had left the door open after stoking the fire with books, and he could feel the heat. Edward kicked the fire door closed and went back to the stairs for further directions. Outside he could hear Fearon's golf cart returning. Adele and Slink were nowhere to be seen.

CHAPTER 20

Edward jumped in the air and turned around all in one move. He dashed back inside the Command Center and pulled the door closed as he went. Inside the Center he looked around in desperation for a solution to his plight. There was only the computer, and that was beginning to look questionable. The fire door beneath the keyboard had bounced back open after he'd kicked it shut and hot coals were spilling out onto the floor. Outside he heard Fearon's golf cart stop in front of the Command Center.

Edward got back on the computer and ran through the steps again, key by key, from CHOICES down to SELECTIONS then to OPTIONS and finally to SECURITY. This time he recognized the tune from his years of weekly piano lessons. The heat on his legs was growing intense, and he was hopping from one foot to the other as he played the finish of the tune, singing along as he went "...and the skies are not cloudy all day,"

The boy could hear Fearon's hurried footsteps starting up the stairs as a list of security sectors came up on the screen. Gnome on the Range was the first one but Edward highlighted all the options and hit "DELETE". There was a pause, and then Security systems all over the massive store began to beep as they shut down. A distant cheer from the direction of Gnome on the Range rose above the hissing noise that was coming from the computer.

Edward could hear Fearon at the top of the stairs and saw the doorknob turn. The boy took the pricer from his pocket and fired. Rather than spitting out a bar code the beam ripped a dollar sign shaped hole in the door. He could hear Fearon the Feared running back down the stairs and starting up his golf cart.

When the cart could no longer be heard, Edward headed for the stairs only to be met by Slink on the landing just outside the door. The Gnome embraced the boy in a bear hug and lifted him off his feet.

"No need for such demonstrations," Edward said.

"You did it my boy," Slink said as he spun them both around.

The celebration came to a sudden stop when a pricer beam shattered the glass window of the door. Slink, caught in mid celebration, carried Edward back into the room, and they both dropped to the floor. The two eased forward and peeked out of the bottom of the doorway and through the balustrade of the stairway. A Jamook in full battle dress was in the plaza below, circling the fountain in his Mookmobile. The creature took aim at the Command Center and fired his weapon. The green dollar sign flashed on the window next to the piano and the glass shattered.

Edward and Slink rolled back into the room. The fire box was aglow, and the coals on the floor had started a smoldering fire that was creeping across the rug. The cast iron was beginning to make popping sounds, and the room smelled of hot metal.

"That thing's hot," Slink said as he quickly pulled away.

"Yes, I may have overloaded the fire box," Edward said as he crawled forward and peered, once again, out the door. "That Jamook is driving circles in the plaza and firing at us every time he comes around this way. He's also eating soda crackers by the hand full and drinking vegetable oil from a gallon jug. And there is Fearon's golf cart. I can just see the nose of it. He must be waiting back on the Mook Trail until he sees how this one is going to end."

"So Fearon didn't go for help. Well, we're OK here. That Jamook can't see us very well, if at all, and Fearon the Fearful isn't going to take any risks. But if we start down these stairs, they have the advantage," Slink said as he crawled up next to Edward to escape the smoke that was beginning to fill the room.

"How long before that Jamook's pricer runs down?" Edward asked as he looked back at the smoldering piano.

"It has a ten-shot battery pack, but he has a charger and a second battery in the cart. That's standard Jamook battlefield equipment. He can fire with one battery while he charges the other. Could go on like that for quite some time," Slink explained.

"Do you think he is driving one of the Mookmobiles that Adele fixed with a Weasel?" Edward asked.

"Could be," Slink said. "I think I recognize that Jamook's bedpan head gear."

Edward jumped up, ran to the wardrobe, took out a pair of Fearon's white gloves, and put them on. Next, he tossed the flowers aside and stuck his hands, one at a time, down into the water in the vase. He poured the rest of the water over his pant legs and then flipped the table on its side. Slink caught on to what was happening and helped the boy push the table up against the bottom of the piano to block the heat.

Edward reached over, turned the microphone on, and twisted the volume up all the way. Steam rose from his gloved fingertips when he touched the metal knob of the mike. A squealing shriek of feedback reverberated throughout STUFF-4-LESS. Edward went back to the front door, took a deep breath of fresh air, stepped back in front of the piano and began to play and sing. Slink began to laugh and sing along as he crawled beneath the smoke and over to the door. The words and music boomed throughout the enormous store.

> All around the cobbler's bench.
> The monkey chased the weasel.
> The monkey thought it was all in fun.
> POP goes the Weasel.

Slink, who was watching the plaza from the door, gave Edward a play-by-play of the action as the last refrain from the song echoed from the speakers throughout the store. "BINGO! Adele's weasel worked. Two blow-outs on the far turn. He's lost control and ran smack into the fountain base. Oooo, vegetable oil all over the place. Not a pretty sight."

Edward dropped down and joined Slink at his observation post just as the computer blew out its small screen. At the bottom of the stairs, he could see Adele spinning doughnut turns in her joy. Across the plaza the creature revved his engine to the max but only succeeded in throwing off shredded tires. "He looks to be dead in the water, but still has a clear shot at us. If we can get to the bottom of these steps, the fountain will be between us and him," Edward said.

The Gnome ducked back into the smoke and came out with one of the mirrored doors from Fearon's wardrobe. "Stay close behind me," he said as he hefted the door in front of them. "Ready, set, go,"

They started down the stairs behind the mirrored door. The Jamook, who had just reloaded a fresh battery into his pricer, began to fire shot after shot in rapid succession. Several shots reflected off the mirror while some hit the staircase. A section of the railing fell away and almost took the friends with it. Edward counted each shot out loud. The tenth and last shot hit the mirror squarely, ricocheted back toward the Jamook and whacked the head clean off Fearon's statue. The stone head landed square on top of the creature's bed pan helmet with a resounding clank. The bed pan was driven firmly down over the Jamook's eyes.

Slink dropped the door, and the two dashed to the bottom of the steps where they joined Adele in the cover of the fountain. The Jamook, in his hurry to reload his pricer with oil covered hands and little or no vision, dropped the fresh battery pack to the ground. The creature reached down as far as he could to feel around for the battery, lost his balance, and tumped over.

"That one is out of action," Slink said. "And it looks like Fearon's gone as well."

"Fearon knows about the portal," Edward said.

"That could be bad if it's true."

"He had Adele's pink cat folder up in his Command Center," Edward said as he looked back up to the top of the steps. Smoke was billowing out of the broken windows.

"The Jamooks must have brought it to him after they destroyed her compound," Slink said as he started down the Mook Highway in the direction from which they had come.

They soon discovered Fearon's golf cart about 20 yards from the plaza. It had multiple flat tires, and Fearon the Feared was gone.

Up ahead, in the direction of Gnome on the Range, the sounds of battle were growing louder. "Fearon is rallying his troupes, but if he fails, I'm afraid he will try to make it to the portal." Slink said. "He and his Jamooks are between us and the Gnomes. It might be best if we circle around and get ourselves between Fearon and his fallback destination."

They ducked down a side road, more of an alley than a Mook Trail, and made their way around piles of discard and destruction. They traveled most of the day without incident although the sounds of battle could be heard in almost every direction. Edward soon lost all his bearings, but Slink made decisions, when decisions needed to be made, with certainty.

Quite often their progress was slowed by landslides of debris, busted Vipers and Hogs. Pathways had to be cleared for Adele. Sometimes they had to stop altogether for Jamooks. Even if the beasts looked dead, they had to be given a wide berth. The need to avoid stepping on sharp Weasel nails was ever present. In places Edward had to take the broom which had served as Adele's arm and sweep the path clear.

It was rapidly growing dark now, and the boy could tell that the fire in Fearon's control center had taken out the STUFF-4-LESS emergency lighting. "How far do you think we are from the portal?" he asked as he sat down on one side of a broken footstool. All around him were furtive sounds coming from the various mounds of junk.

"This looks like as good a place to camp as any," Slink said as he pulled two cans of condensed soup from his backpack and held them up so Edward could see the labels. "Bean with bacon or clam chowder?" Slink asked.

Edward pointed listlessly toward one of the cans. Slink peeled back the top of the container, stuck a spoon in the congealed chowder, and handed it to Edward.

"As to your question about the portal, I have no answer for that," Slink said as he sat down on the other edge of the stool and began to spoon thick, cold soup into his mouth. "Truth is, I'm totally lost. Have been for quite some time."

Edward looked out at the growing darkness and thought about his home. He thought about how much he missed his old life, his father, and yes, even his brother Clemens.

Slink seemed to sense his friend's despair. "Don't worry, we'll find our way back to the portal," he said. "Why, I'm sure we'll all be at you house in plenty of time for Thanksgiving."

The boy made no reply.

CHAPTER 21

They awoke at first light and set out again. Within a few hundred yards they found themselves on the edge of a large open space that was littered with abandoned Mookmobiles, empty inflatable wading pool boxes, tanks of helium and a stack of blow-up pumpkins waiting to be inflated.

In the center of the room was a launch pad. Laid out on the pad was a plastic pool, complete with box fan and car battery. It was ready and waiting to be filled with helium. A forklift was parked nearby. Sharp nails from the Weasels littered the floor.

"This must be where they launched the airborne strike," Edward said as he checked the gauges on one of the helium canisters. "They used the forklift to take the Jamooks out of their carts and load them into the pools. That's why there are so many carts around here but none of those creatures."

"If we can find enough of that helium to fill a kiddy pool, we might get airborne ourselves," Slink said as he looked into the empty pool boxes. "Once I'm up in the air, I'm sure I'll be able to get my bearings."

"There are plenty of inflatable pumpkins here, and it looks like many of these tanks still have some gas in them." Edward said as he took the broom and began to sweep a trail free of nails, "but the only pool seems to be the one in the center and that one has at least four Weasel nails sticking out of it that I can see. The Jamooks were long gone when the Weasels on all these carts popped. There must have been nails flying everywhere."

While the boy and the Gnome were inspecting the damaged pool, Adele pulled up beside them. She studied the situation with her cameras and did some calculations which sounded, to Edward, like coffee percolating. Her printer came to life and spat out a small page of peel-and-stick bar code labels. Slink peeled the paper free from the backing, pulled the nails out of the side of the pool, and slapped the labels over the holes. They made a tight seal.

They rolled the robot into the middle of the pool and began to inflate the craft with helium from the tanks. When it was half full of the buoyant gas, they checked the pool for additional leaks. There were a few which were quickly repaired with Adele's patches. Edward found a spool of heavy cord and began inflating pumpkins and fastening them around the edge of the pool.

"Make sure those pumpkin rope knots are secure," Slink said as he tied two ropes across the top of the craft so it wouldn't take off until the crew was all aboard.

"I got my merit badge in knot tying just last month," Edward said as he gave each knot an extra loop and a tug.

"How much weight do you think we can carry?" Slink asked.

Adele's printer hummed into action and spit out a page which Slink read out loud. "A Jamook in full battle dress weighs somewhere in the neighborhood of 330 pounds."

"I'm about 75 pounds," the boy said. "How much do you weigh?" he asked Slink and Adele.

"About 60 pounds for me," Slink answered, "But I'm sure I lost a few pounds on this adventure what with the irregular meals and such."

Adele's screen blushed red. "A lady's weight is a private matter," Slink explained. "I think you can safely say our total, including the battery and the fan, would be somewhere around 250."

Edward climbed out of the pool and began to sweep up nails. He borrowed Adele's dustpan and scooped the nails into doubled up shopping bags. "I'd say we can take about 30 pounds of these and two or three of those helium tanks, whichever are the fullest. These might come in handy, and we'll still be well below Jamook fighting weight."

Edward tested the box fan while Slink topped off the helium in the pool. The craft pulled hard on its mooring ropes. "We will have to release both ropes at the same time, so we get a smooth launch," Slink said to Edward as they joined Adele in the pool.

The boy got a grip on the end of the rope on the port side, and the Gnome grabbed the one to starboard. "On my count now," Slink said. "One.. and a Two.. and a Three...."

With the release of the mooring ropes the gas filled pool rocked from side to side. The boy and the Gnome staggered as they tried to regain their balance while Adele, using her various arms as stabilizers, centered herself in the craft. The airship evened out and began to rise steadily. Slink and Edward tried to find their sea legs while laughing and executing a clumsy high-five.

"I suppose we should keep an eye out for drones, but I don't see any," Edward said.

"I've been seeing downed Vipers and Hogs a lot since we left Fearon's Command Center. My guess is the drones were controlled by that old, coal fired computer. When the computer went down, so did the drones," Slink said

The wading pool rose higher and higher while the view opened up before them. Fearon's command post was just below. A column of smoke rose from the broken windows and out through a crack in the distant ceiling. They watched as the Command Center exploded sending the sheet metal chimney skyward like a rocket.

"We were traveling in circles," Edward said as he switched on the box fan and angled it to turn the air ship. The pool swept in a gentle arc as it rose even higher.

A flock of flamingos circled the craft. "Look at those beauties," Slink said as he pulled the Christmas stocking off of his hat and tossed it overboard.

Edward laughed and pulled the wreath from his head and the artificial pine boughs from his body. He sent them flying after Slink's makeshift Santa hat. Slink peeled off his red shirt, dropped it to the floor and did a horn pipe on top of it. The two friends removed Adele's disguise as well.

"Do you know which way it is to the portal?" Edward asked as he took control of the fan once again.

"Let me see," Slink said as he peered into the distance. "I think I see the remains of the Jamook hatchery, and that open space next to it must be Gnome on the Range. Bring her around to the starboard," he said as he pointed to the left.

The ship tilted as Edward changed direction, and the metal waste basket that was part of Adele's Jamook costume rolled up against Slink's legs. He picked up the can along with the mop head wig and was about to toss them up and over the ring of inflatable pumpkins and then stopped in mid throw, his mouth open.

"And the ceiling is right there," Edward said as he followed Slink's gaze.

Not only was the craft still rising, but it seemed to be picking up speed. It was heading toward a hole in the roof where the serrated edges of a shattered plastic skylight jutted out like the teeth in a shark's mouth. "We have to get rid of some of these pumpkins. You untie one on your side, I'll untie one over here," Slink said as he labored with the knot on the pumpkin nearest to him. "What kind of knot is this, anyway?"

"It's a double running bowline," Edward answered as he struggled with the knot on his side as well.

"How do you get them loose?" Slink said in frustration.

"I don't know. I think we were going to learn to untie knots next month." Edward said as he inspected a broken fingernail. "What happens if we go out through the hole?"

"No one knows," Slink said as he looked up at the jagged opening. "And I don't reckon it really matters. Looks to me like we're heading for a shredding."

CHAPTER 22

SSSSSSSSS....

Adele peeled back the patch from the biggest hole in the wading pool and the helium began to escape in a strong, steady stream. The escaping gas propelled the craft away from the jagged hole. The rate of ascent slowed until the inflated pumpkins bumped softly against the roof. The vessel began to gently fall. When it reached an altitude well below the roofline, the robot resealed the hole, and the pool stabilized.

Adele ran a page out of her printer, and Slink read it. "We will be cruising today at 75 feet, well above the range of Jamook pricers. Our arrival time will depend entirely on where we are going." On her monitor a perky flight attendant appeared in a powder blue suit and matching pillbox hat.

Edward took over at the controls, directing the fan and the airship while Slink moved to the prow and tried to get his bearings once again. "Bring it around to the port," Slink said while pointing to the right.

Edward saw no reason to correct Slink and angled the fan accordingly. The ship moved in a slow, lazy arc.

"That's got her," Slink said when they had reached the desired heading. "Full speed ahead."

Edward straightened the fan, turned the dial up to high, and settled back against the rim of the pool. Full speed for a wading pool airship is not very fast, but the boy didn't mind. It was a beautiful day in STUFF-4-LESS with shafts of sunlight slanting down through the skylights. There was a gentle breeze blowing on his face and the air smelled clear and fresh.

In a short while Slink got Edward's attention and pointed down. Below them was Gnome on the Range and the Jamook Incubator. Activity was everywhere. Slink twirled his finger in the air, and the boy angled the fan to set the ship in a circling pattern.

On the ground, Gnomes were taking down the fence around Gnome on the Range, building street barricades and loading dead Jamooks into the Mook Mincer with the aid of the forklift. When they saw the shadow of the swimming pool pass overhead, they scurried for cover. Slink took hold of one of the pumpkin ropes, stepped up onto the rim of the pool, and waved. The Gnomes below recognized him, and a roar went up so loud that Slink almost lost his balance.

Edward turned the fan off and the ship drifted to a stop. Gnomes gathered and cheered. Clink, Slink's sister, climbed up on the old observation stand and held up her arms to silence the crowd. When all was quiet, she shouted up to her brother. "Can you see the Jamook army from up there?"

Adele ran the lenses on her cameras out to maximum telephoto and scanned the horizon. At one point she stopped, made a clicking sound, and printed out a photo of a distant area marked with a bull's-eye.

Edward could tell the photo was taken with an infrared filter.

Slink took the photo and looked it over. "There's an unexplained heat signature about a mile or so from here. We'll check it out," he reported. "Have you seen Fearon?"

"There were reports of him trying to sneak by the flamingos. You know how territorial those birds can get. They worked him over pretty well, but it's believed he made it past," Clink said. "You find that army, you'll find Fearon."

Edward turned the fan back on and set it on high while Slink held his place in the front of the craft. The boy held steady with only minor adjustments in accordance with Slink's hand signals. In time he could see, off to their left, the cloud of blue smoke which had registered on the infrared film. The smoke was moving, slowly but steadily, toward their position.

"That looks like the Jamook Army on the move," Slink said. "Perhaps we should avoid them if we can."

The boy angled the fan and brought the airship directly in line with the moving column of exhaust fumes.

Slink smiled back at the boy with pride. "On second thought, let's take it to them head on."

In a short while Edward began to feel a vibration in the pit of his stomach, and then he heard a low growl which grew steadily louder. They cleared a rubbish hill, and saw, just ahead of them, the Jamook Army rolling through a narrow canyon. The column of Mookmobiles, three abreast, stretched back along the highway for a hundred yards or more. "Every Mookmobile in STUFF-4-LESS must be here," Edward said.

"Every cart that Adele didn't stick a Weasel under," Slink added.

The lead vehicles were lawn tractors mounted with powerful leaf blowers that swung back and forth sweeping debris and Weasel nails from the path as they came. All the Jamooks were heavily armed. At the back of the column Fearon rode in a regal throne fashioned from a Lazy Boy and mounted high, but unsteadily, on a motorized wheelchair.

On his head Fearon the Feared sported a bright yellow bicycle helmet with orange butterfly decals. He wore football shoulder pads over his suit jacket and soccer shin guards over his pants. He held an aluminum tee-ball bat tucked under his arm like a swagger stick.

"Swing it around, and come at them from the front," Slink said as he scrambled to replace Adele's Jamook wig and tin waste basket on her head. "Let's see your best Jamook face now."

Adele moved up to the bow of the craft and flashed a big Jamook smile while Edward made some final adjustments to bring the ship in high over the front of the column. The Jamooks, thinking the floating pool was one of their own, cheered and waved their webbed hands. Edward and slink, hidden beneath the rim of the pool, waved back with the broom and dustpan.

By the time the army below realized their mistake it was too late. Edward and Slink jumped up and poured a steady rain of Weasel nails down over the front part of the column just behind the row of sweepers. The sound of bursting tires, overloaded with the weight of Jamooks, echoed like gun shots in the canyon. Carts swerved into other carts; wheels locked up; and Mookmobiles overturned, dumping creatures out onto the road. In no time the highway was clogged, bringing the Jamook Army to a standstill.

Fearon began to shout commands, trying to organize a defense. Some of the Jamook Mobiles were fitted with ball launchers, the type Edward had seen being used on tennis courts for practice sessions. These ball launchers had a small flame burning on the end of the tube, and the balls, soaked in lighter fluid, ignited as they were launched. Flaming tennis balls whizzed around the floating wading pool with one knocking the metal waste basket hat off Adele's monitor. The ball fell to the floor of the craft. Slink quickly picked up the basket and used it to scoop up the flaming tennis ball and dump it overboard.

    Edward continued to rain Weasel nails down on the Jamook army. Their ship, as it grew lighter, rose again toward the ceiling. Adele opened the patch and let helium escape to compensate for the loss of weight.

    Jamooks fired their pricers, but the airship was well out of range. The beams, diffused by distance, only managed to bathe the craft in an eerie green light. Some Jamooks managed to fire arrows with road flairs taped to the shaft up at the aircraft overhead. But the projectiles fell short and only succeeded in setting fire to the gas that was leaking from the overturned carts. The smell of burning gasoline and sulfur wafted up from the valley floor.

The three friends had run the length of the Jamook column, raining down Weasels nails, and were now directly above Fearon in his mobile throne. Slink and Edward hefted one of the helium tanks to the bow of the pool and tipped it over the side. As the heavy tank fell the front of the pool bounced up. Both Edward and Slink fell back on the seat of their pants. They jumped back up and went to see if their efforts were rewarded. They leaned over the bow of the craft and looked below. The tank had scored a direct hit, crushing its way down through the seat of the chair. Springs and foam padding were sticking out everywhere, but Fearon was gone.

 They looked back over the once formidable attack force. The Jamook army was in complete disarray. Many Mookmobiles were disabled, and more than a few were on fire. Fat and lumbering creatures worked to free themselves from overturned carts. One particularly large Jamook near the end of the column aimed a powerful crossbow and sent a flared arrow up toward the retreating aircraft. Slink, Edward and Adele watched as the bolt flew high above the pool and struck a bank of florescent lights up near the ceiling. There was a ball of flame as the flare and lights exploded. Glass shards and fiery fragments rained down toward the floating airship.

CHAPTER 23

Edward picked up the discarded shirt from Slink's Santa costume and tried to brush the hot splinters off the plastic pool and pumpkin heads before they did any real damage. Slink removed Adele's Jamook wig and began to do the same. When they had cleared all the embers they could reach, Slink once again looked around and got his bearings.

"Bring her around to port," he said as he pointed to the right. "I see the area where the portal is; I'm almost sure of it."

Edward manned the box fan once again and set a course in the direction of the portal. They soon left the valley with the devastated Jamook army behind them. The craft had just cleared the ridge that defined the valley when they heard an explosion followed by a second and a third. Black smoke rose above the mountain of trash, and then all was quiet. No more Jamook war whoops or the sound of revving engines.

The only sound that could be heard was a slight hissing.

"We're leaking!" Edward cried.

Adele began to spit out bar-code stickers as fast as she could while Slink and Edward peeled them from their backing and stuck them over the countless pinholes made by the glass shards and embers. Despite all their effort they could feel the floating craft slowly sinking.

Edward and Slink rolled the two remaining helium tanks into place and began to re-inflate the pool. The tanks did some good but soon ran out. They heaved the empty canisters over the side. With the fresh helium and without the weight of the gas tanks the airship rose enough to clear the next mountain range.

Adele soon ran out of patches and the air ship began to slowly drop, getting closer to the jagged peaks below. After a while Edward had to steer around the mounds rather than going over them. The floating pool slowly sank until it was down so low the boy had to follow the Mook Trails. Their air speed dropped as the ship became less and less buoyant. Finally, with the craft almost at a standstill and hovering just above the road surface, Edward cut the fan. The pool settled gently to the ground.

"Fine landing, my boy," Slink said with pride. "We can walk to the portal from here."

"How far is it?" The boy asked.

"About a quarter mile, maybe a little more," Slink said as he pointed out the remains of Topside hanging from the roof in the distance. "Don't worry. This part of the store I know quite well."

Slink and Edward stood on one edge of the rapidly shrinking pool and compressed it down enough so Adele could roll out over it. "Do you really think Fearon is going to try to get to the Portal?" Edward asked.

"He has no reason to stay here and every reason to leave. The Jamook Army is in ruins, and every Gnome in STUFF-4-LESS is out looking for him.

And don't forget, there's a good chance he originally came from that side," Slink replied. "He'll be heading to the Portal sure enough. It will be trouble for BUY-N-BULK if he makes it. Let's just hope that we get there first."

As they approached the entrance to the cooler Slink halted the group behind an outcropping of twisted baby carriages and strollers at the edge of Baby Supplies. A flock of flamingos circled overhead. "Those birds might be trying to tell us something," he said.

"Do you think the birds mean Fearon is near?" Edward asked.

"Could be," Slink replied. "Could mean nothing at all. Flamingos are good company and make good pets, but they are frequently unreliable. Let's hide and watch for a while."

They held their position and after a while the birds left. "I guess we're going to have to go in there some time, it may as well be now," Slink said as he stepped out from behind the heap of ruined baby accessories.

The door to the cooler stood open just as it was when they left. Inside the dead Jamook had been removed, but his motorized cart was still there up against the door on the far end, the door back to Edward's home. The only thing they could see that was different was the shiny new padlock and hasp that had been fastened to that far door. It was attached with large nails driven halfway in and then bent over.

"That looks like Jamook craftsmanship," Edward said.

"Let's move the Mookmobile and see about opening the door," Slink said. They tried to push the machine but, even though it still had all its tires inflated, it wouldn't budge.

"It must be in gear," Edward said as he climbed up into the seat and looked over the controls.

"Can we get it away from the door?" Slink asked.

"My father has been teaching me how to drive the riding lawn mower back home," Edward said as he pulled out the choke. He depressed the clutch with his foot and turned the key. The engine sputtered as it sucked gas back into its carburetor and then caught. The boy revved the engine and smiled triumphantly.

"Well done for a BUY-N-BULKer," came a voice from behind the door they had entered. It was the same dark and threatening voice that had been heard coming over the PA system in STUFF-4-LESS. Fearon the Feared, his clothes and hair bird-pecked and spattered, stood in the doorway and leveled his pricer at Edward. The voice, with all its rasping, loudspeaker qualities, came directly from the little man.

Slink, who was caught in the act of squirting an aerosol can of whipped cream into his mouth, mumbled defiantly.

"And you, you wretched little creature. You cost me my empire." Fearon said as he used the aluminum ball bat in his left hand to brush a pink flamingo feather away from in front of his eyes. He swung the pricer in his right hand around in the direction of Slink.

"He isn't a wretched little creature. He's my friend," Edward Eliot Emmons said.

Edward was surprised by the force in his own voice. Everything seemed to stop, and the cooler room fell silent.

One heartbeat, two heart beats, and then things happened. Many things, and they all seemed to happen at once.

Edward popped the clutch on the Mookmobile. Fearon swung his pricer up at Edward, but just as he pulled the trigger, a gallon jug of milk fell from the highest shelf and landed squarely on top of the evil man's head.

The machine lurched forward, and the boy tumbled over backwards and out of the seat. The green dollar sign beam missed his head by inches and burned a hole through the pad lock on the BUY-N-BULK door. The smoking lock and hasp fell to the floor in pieces.

Fearon looked up to see where the milk jug had come from just as Clemens Emmons pushed another gallon off the shelf. The jug hit the bean counter right in the face and burst open. The bean counter dropped his weapon, and it bounced to the side. Slink made a dive for it and belly-flopped into a pool of milk.

The driver-less Mookmobile lurched forward with its razor-sharp woodchipper blades spinning. Slink scrambled out of the way but Fearon, felled by the second milk jug blow, was scooped up by the woodchipper's hopper. The Mookmobile, Fearon and the chipper rumbled out the STUFF-4-LESS door and down the Mook trail.

When things had settled, Clemens flipped down off the top shelf, swung briefly from one hand like an ape and dropped lightly to the floor.

"That," Edward said, "is my little brother, Clemens."

Slink picked him up in a bear hug and swung him around until Clemens was dizzy.

"That's Slink. He's a hugger," Edward explained when the Gnome had finally put the little brother down. "And this is Adele." The robot hugged Clemens with one arm that looked like a pair of Vice Grip pliers and another arm that looked like the boom of a toy steam shovel.

"Pleased to meet you," Clemens uttered.

"How long have you been up there on that shelf in the cooler?" Edward asked.

"I just got here," Clemens explained. "Dad sent me to see what was taking you so long."

Edward was puzzled by this. He worked the math on his fingers. "How can that be. I've been gone for several days and you just got here."

Adele began to whir, and a sheet of paper shot out of her printer port. Slink took it and began to read.

"According to Adele's calculations, STUFF-4-LESS time and BUY-N-BULK time are not sinkharoo..., sickcron...

Edward took the page and continued the reading. "They are not synchronized. Just a few minutes in BUY-N-BULK can be a few days in STUFF-4-LESS and vice versa. Your visit to STUFF-4-LESS did not take away from your BUY-N-BULK time."

Clemens and Slink were passing the can of whipped cream back and forth, filling their mouths and then puffing out their cheeks.

"I don't know anything about STUFF-4-LESS time, but I do know if I don't get you back to BUY-N-BULK right away, Dad will blow a gasket," Clemens said through a mouthful of topping. "He's already pretty upset over a little mishap we had with a pumpkin."

"I really must go," Edward said to Slink and Adele. He gave them each a big hug. "Do you think there is any chance you could join us for Thanksgiving?"

"Thanksgiving at your house sounds wonderful, but we have much work to do right here in our own land, "Slink said as he took off his hat and rung some more milk out of it. "But we Gnomes are all for one and one for all once again and, with both Fearon and the Jamook army in shreds, I am sure we will triumph. It's just a matter of time."

"I wish I could stay and help," Edward said with Clemens tugging at his sleeve.

"You've done more than enough already," Slink said as he replaced his damp hat on his head. "Rest assured, the first thing we will do after our victory is to tear down the headless statue of Fearon in the Plaza and erect one to a real hero."

"I'm really not a hero," Edward protested.

"You drove right into Fearon's line of fire. Right into the barrel of his pricer." Slink said through a mouthful of whipped cream. "If that's not a hero I don't know what is."

"I only did it because you told me Fearon's pricer only set prices and didn't fire green laser beams."

"Did I say that?" Slink said. "My bad. Still, what you did adds up to hero in my book."

Adele produced a camera and began snapping photos of Edward. She extended a telescoping arm to get several different angles. The robot then pulled the group together and took a dozen selfies.

"By this time next year we will be having a Thanksgiving dinner of our own, and you will be the guest of honor," Slink concluded.

"I would like that. I would like that very much," Edward said.

Clemens climbed up on Edward's shoulders and undid the latch on the cooler door that led back to BUY-N-BULK. Adele produced a short but stout fishing rod with a large magnet for a hook. She cast the magnet out and stuck it to the metal door which she reeled open. The robot had a tear in the big eye she displayed on her monitor.

"Goodbye Edward, my boy, I am sure we will be seeing you again," Slink said with a catch in his throat.

As the two boys passed through the open door, the Gnome called out, "Edward, Clemens, don't forget the milk."

THE END

Made in United States
Orlando, FL
19 November 2024